I0557848

MADDY MADRIGAL MYSTERIES BOOK 3

DESPERATE MAGIC

DEBRA CASTANEDA

SHADOW CANYON
— press —

ISBN: 979-8-9903956-9-5
Edited by: Lyndsey Smith, Horrorsmith Editing
Cover design by: Jacqueline Sweet

To Lyndsey Smith, my extraordinary editor

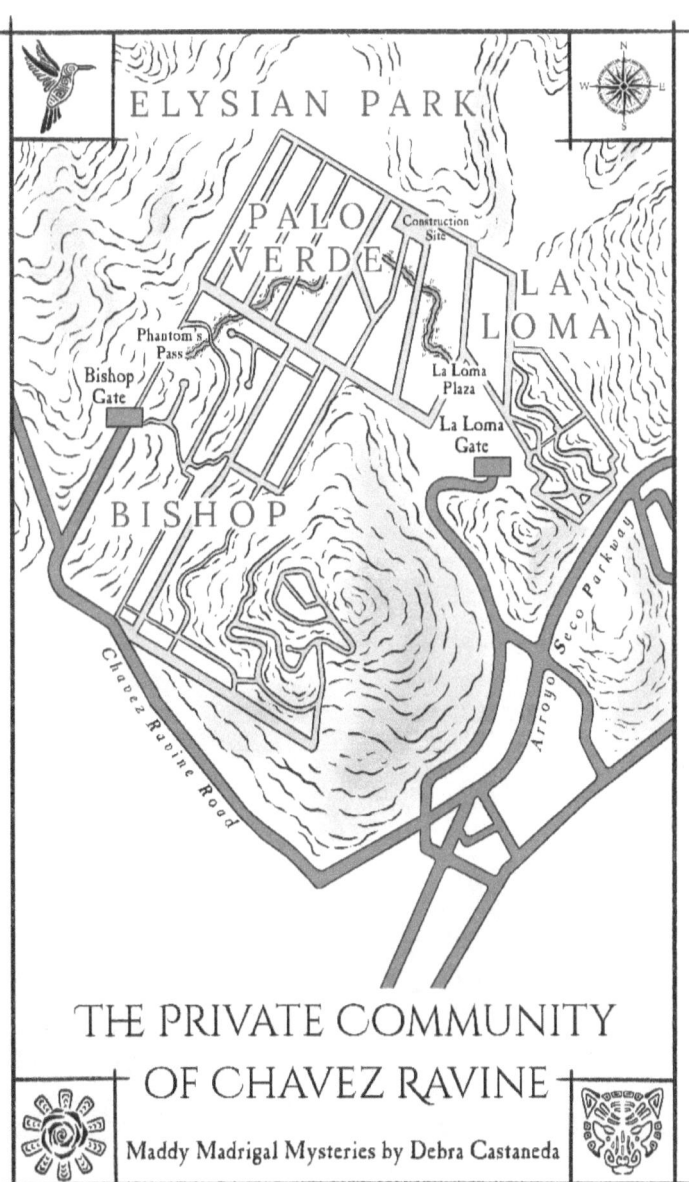

ELYSIAN PARK

PALO VERDE

Construction Site

LA LOMA

Phantom's Pass

Bishop Gate

La Loma Plaza

La Loma Gate

BISHOP

Chavez Ravine Road

Arroyo Seco Parkway

THE PRIVATE COMMUNITY
OF CHAVEZ RAVINE

Maddy Madrigal Mysteries by Debra Castaneda

Chapter 1

There was a reason I never considered a career as a homicide detective, and it was lying on the floor of a beautiful Spanish-style home.

Throw any kind of shrieking, spitting, hairy entity at me and I would be fine, but a body? Yuck.

When I first took the job as head of security for the Chavez Ravine Homeowners Association, murder had been the least of my worries. Entity eruptions and board politics were the things that kept me up at night.

But the unthinkable happened, and according to the people who found the body, the victim had met a brutal and horrific end.

I had been at a party when I got the call. One of my security officers, Ron Mendez, whisked me to the scene in his marked vehicle. I thanked him for the ride, got out, and stared at the house.

Ornamental streetlamps broke the darkness of the summer night. The landscaping was lush, the palm trees majestic. Crickets and a few birds provided a soundtrack for the calm setting.

But there had been no peace for the home's owner.

Brandon, a sturdy young security officer who had encountered his fair share of terrifying creatures in his short career, stood on the lawn, pale as a sheet of paper. And then there was Becca Tey. The actress paced back and forth on the driveway, trembling as though it were freezing, not a warm, still evening.

"I can't believe it," she kept repeating. "Who would do that? *What* would do that? It had to be some sort of animal."

Or entity, I thought. A chill ran up my spine. Chavez Ravine had been entity-free ever since I managed to cast a protection spell over the community.

I walked over to Brandon, staying on the pavement due to my heels. "Any sign of a break-in?"

He shook his head and pointed to the side yard. A tall hedge separated the victim's house from the Craftsman-style home next door.

"No forced entry as far as I can tell, but there's an open window around back."

The house was situated on a cul-de-sac with three other homes. A hill loomed above the dead-end street, and at the summit of the tree-lined ridge stood Elysian Park—a favorite entity hangout. The proximity of the park to the murder scene made me nervous for a whole bunch of reasons.

Several neighbors were outside on their front porches, but for now, they were staying there, thanks to Ron. He spoke with them in hushed tones, trying to gather as much information as he could before we ceded control to the LAPD.

"You didn't touch the window, did you?" I asked Brandon.

He raked a hand through his hair. "Course not. I touched the lady's neck to see if she had a pulse, but I was real careful not to touch anything else."

"You wouldn't happen to have any plastic bags in your vehicle, would you?"

Brandon arched his eyebrows. The guy was smart. He knew exactly what I had in mind.

"As a matter of fact, I do." He jutted his chin out at the neighbors. "Those people will see what you're doing."

I thought for a moment.

"Not if you go over there and tell everyone we're calling the police and they need to wait inside. Tell them it's going to be a long night and there won't be anything to see anyway."

Technically, I had *no* business going inside. I might have been head of security for the gated community in the hills above Los Angeles, but my job had its limits. Homicide was the exclusive domain of the LAPD.

Which was going to be a problem.

The police and the residents of Chavez Ravine had gone through a major rough patch many years ago, when the cops enforced the city's eviction order. The passage of time hadn't even put a dent in the resentment seething just below the surface. The board—my bosses—had instructed me to keep the cops out of the three neighborhoods that made up Chavez Ravine, no matter what.

Which was a fine policy for the occasional car break-in, but not when someone found a dead body. I was going to have to call the police and deal with the board later.

But first, I had a little business to conduct, so I headed for the front door.

I was, after all, the head of security. And the board would have questions, which I had better have answers for. Plus, I was an ex-cop, so investigating came naturally.

And that was how I rationalized my decision to enter a crime scene I knew was off-limits.

Brandon fetched a box of latex gloves and a roll of black plastic bags from the back of his vehicle. While he sauntered over to deal with the neighbors, I tugged on the gloves and pulled the bags over my heels, securing them around my ankles with rubber bands.

Becca hurried over. "You don't want to go in there."

"Maybe not, but I need to see this for myself." I paused. "How *did* you happen to find her?"

Becca was around fifty, and the plastic surgery she'd had over the years wasn't aging gracefully. Still, with her flashing dark eyes and long black hair, she was a striking woman.

She sniffed loudly. "We've known each other forever. Her name is Misty Denner. She's a character actor. A really good one. Unlike me, she gets lots of work." There was no trace of bitterness in Becca's voice, just admiration. "She broke her ankle last week on a shoot, so I came over with a bottle of wine and some snacks to keep her company. We were going to watch a movie together."

Misty Denner. I vaguely recognized the name. "Okay. I'm going to take a quick look around, then I'll be right back."

She gave a curt nod and looked away.

I had first met Becca when I was fresh on the job and we were dealing with some scary supernatural creatures. Becca was quirky and had a few bad habits, but she was honest and thoughtful, and I liked her.

"I think I'll go throw up in the bushes again," she said in a small voice.

I thought she was joking, but while I walked across the wide porch, the sounds coming from the hedge told me she was not.

The front door was open. Brandon had used the emergency code on the pin pad next to the mailbox.

The moment I crossed the threshold, a pungent odor invaded my nostrils. At first, I assumed something in the kitchen had gone bad, but after a few more sniffs, I decided it smelled more like wet, stinky dog.

The house was twice as big as mine, if not larger, but still smaller than many of the others in Chavez Ravine. Misty had leaned into Bohemian decor, with teal-painted walls, a mishmash of furniture, an enormous zebra-striped rug, and a smattering of brightly colored floor pillows. Two table lamps lit the room.

I took it all in—very artsy, very much like the woman in the framed photos on the wall. Misty Denner had played quirky, oddball roles on TV and in the movies for years.

Vases of fresh flowers crowded a tile-topped sofa table, along with get-well cards, probably for the broken ankle.

I peered into the kitchen. The lamplight didn't reach quite that far, but from what I could make out, it was clean. No lingering cooking odors. A pizza box sitting on top of a trash can suggested Misty had chosen well. Agostino's at La Loma Plaza made a mean pie.

The hall was long and dim, with a faint light coming from a room toward the end.

I swallowed hard, dreading what came next. *Just take a quick look and get the hell out.* Just a peek to see what we were dealing with—thirty seconds, max—then I would call the police like a good girl.

If I could deal with entities and monsters, there was no need to freak out about a body, right?

I forced my shoulders back and took a deep breath. The plastic bags on my feet crinkled while I walked toward the light.

Within seconds, I was standing outside the murder room, looking through the doorway and trying to take it all in.

A bedside table illuminated the scene.

Misty Denner was crumpled on the floor at the foot of the bed, head bent at an unnatural angle, her small face bruised. She was wearing shorts and a loose shirt, her thin arms and legs covered in what appeared to be bitemarks. Her flesh was smeared with blood.

5

She was a tiny thing, with shoulder-length brown hair that appeared dyed. If I hadn't known she was around fifty, I would have guessed I was looking at a teenager.

The foul, musty odor I had noticed when I first entered the house became a thick stench in the bedroom, and it made me gag.

I covered my nose and dragged my eyes away from the body.

The casement window was large and wide-open. Of course it was—we hadn't had an entity in Chavez Ravine for some time, and violent crime was unheard-of in our community.

Was.

An attacker could have climbed through the window easily. A book on the floor near the nightstand suggested Misty had been reading in bed when he did. Or *it*.

Probably *it*. This was no ordinary homicide.

My heart sank. The protection spell I had cast to keep Chavez Ravine safe from entities must have failed, letting in whatever monster had done this to poor Misty Denner.

Reluctantly, I picked up my phone and dialed 911.

Chapter 2

I needed to make a couple of calls. Once the police arrived, I would be busy providing them with background information and maybe explaining our entity experiences, so I stood on the front porch and took out my phone.

My first call should have been to the HOA board president, but that was going to be awkward, what with me calling in the cops, so I chickened out and rang Julia Suarez instead. Julia was my best friend in Chavez Ravine. She lived not far from me in La Loma, alone, unless her new boyfriend happened to be staying over.

"Hey there!" she answered. "How was the party? Did Stu go? Are you calling to tell me you guys finally did the deed?"

I swallowed. "No. As a matter of fact, I had to leave early." I kicked a little pebble across the pavement and into the lawn. "Listen, Julia…Don't say anything to anyone, but I need you to make sure all your doors and windows are locked. As in, hang up and go do it right now, okay?"

Julia cleared her throat. "Why? What happened? Did more entities show up? I thought you said they can't get inside buildings."

"They can't, unless something's changed. All I can say for now is a woman was killed in La Loma, and I think her attacker got in through an open window. The police are coming, and I need to go handle things, but I'll call you as soon as I can, okay?"

"You're kidding? A murder? Here? That's impossible…Wait…Are you going to send out one of those community alerts to warn people?"

Fair question. It did seem like the right thing to do, but it wasn't my decision to make. I couldn't prove there was an active threat, so the HOA Board would have the final say.

"Julia, I gotta go. Cora needs to know what happened."

I hung up and called HOA President Cora Bernal. She had been at the party when I got the notification about a body, so I was sure she was waiting for me to fill her in.

Cora picked up immediately. "Is it true? Is someone dead?"

"Unfortunately, yes. And Cora, it was bad. *Very* bad. And very likely a homicide."

"Oh, my."

I didn't think she had been expecting that.

Now came the tricky part. "Cora, I called the police—"

She interrupted with a loud gasp. "No! We don't need them here. You're in charge of security. You can handle it. You know what to do. You were a police officer and—"

It was my turn to interrupt.

"If I so much as touch that body, I'll be guilty of interfering with a police investigation. And just imagine the liability if the victim's relatives accuse the HOA of getting in the way of justice for their loved one."

I let that sink in for about five seconds.

"I'm sorry if I sound harsh, Cora, but we don't have a choice this time. They should be here soon, so I need to get going. I'll call you as soon as I have an update. Until then, do you think we should send a note to the owners, letting them know what happened? People should close their windows tonight. Maybe the board would consider sending something out."

That would keep them busy.

"Yes, we'll see about that. Maddy, who died?" Cora's voice was tense. "What do I say to the board?"

"Keep it simple. Just say a woman was found dead in La Loma and an investigation is underway."

Cora gave an aggrieved sigh. "All right…But I wish you could tell me more."

I wished I could too, but that would have meant admitting I had tromped through a crime scene. And if I identified the name of the victim, there was a good chance Cora would tell the other board members. Soon, everyone would be talking about it, *before* the LAPD had a chance to issue a press release, which they would absolutely do. Just like the emergence of entities in entity-free Chavez Ravine, a murder in crime-free Chavez Ravine would be big news.

"Good luck, Cora." I meant it. She was a smart, successful, kind woman, and her role as board president put her in some awkward situations.

I reached down to slip my phone into the pocket of my trench coat and was surprised to discover I wasn't wearing one. My brain was buried in my job, but my body was in a blue cocktail dress.

Lights flashed at the entrance to the cul-de-sac. Three patrol vehicles appeared, followed by a silver muscle car I instantly recognized.

Homicide Detective Leesa Bevlov was the only one on the force who would opt for such a ludicrous ride.

Usually, patrol officers arrived first and then the medical examiner. After all the grunt work was done, the homicide detective would show up. Eventually.

But not this time. This was the LAPD's first opportunity to get into Chavez Ravine in many a decade, and apparently, they were anxious to look around.

The squad cars pulled to the curb. Leesa Bevlov's teen boy dream machine rumbled to a stop in the street.

While the officers hurried toward the house, where Brandon and Ron waited in the front yard, Bevlov got out and leaned against the door, watching. After a moment, she shifted her attention to me and sauntered over, hands stuck into the pockets of her yellow jacket.

"Can I help you with something?" Her voice was flat, disinterested, and slightly nasal.

Oh, hello to you too. "Nice to see you again, Leesa. Actually, I was thinking that, as head of security here, *I* might be able to help *you.*"

Leesa tilted her head and stared. She was a tall and fit woman, mid-forties, with dyed black hair that made her look hard. The black eyeliner didn't help either. "Well, I've been at this a long time, so I doubt it. But if I think of anything, I'll be sure to reach out. In the meantime, I need you and your guards to leave my crime scene alone. Nobody crosses the yellow tape, got it?"

She turned and walked toward the Denner house.

"You can leave your contact information with my partner."

Wow. I bit the inside of my cheek so hard I tasted blood.

Before I worked in Occult Affairs, I had been a patrol officer and had met Bevlov a few times. There wasn't anything in our past I could think of that would explain her icy attitude. I had suspected the LAPD wouldn't play nice, but I hadn't anticipated being frozen out so soon or so completely.

The officers swarmed the house, setting up crime scene tape and questioning Brandon and Ron. Becca sat in her SUV, nibbling a sandwich and staring blankly ahead.

Leesa disappeared into the house. A few officers established the perimeter, silent while they worked.

Moments later, a middle-aged bald guy hurried over and introduced himself as Jeff, Leesa's partner. I didn't recognize him, but he was friendly enough. After he had finished writing down my details, he said, "So, you're head of security? Nice gig. Did you know the victim?"

I shook my head. "No, but her name was Misty Denner. She was a character actress of some renown. Her friend found her and phoned it in. That's Becca Tey sitting over in that car, waiting for someone to take her statement."

"Did this Misty actress live alone?"

"I believe so, but you can confirm that with Becca."

Jeff nodded. "Thanks. I'll go talk to her." He paused. "Hey. I recognize you from that Bad Pete video. That was really something."

He raised his hand into a fist and paused.

Could he really be trying to fist bump? At our age?

Yes, he was. I tapped his fist with mine and made a little face.

"Awesome sauce!" he said, then headed toward Becca.

I couldn't imagine Leesa getting along with someone like that.

Bevlov might have dismissed me, but I still had a job to do. If she was too proud to take advantage of my knowledge of the community, that was her problem.

I walked back to Ron's SUV. If this was an entity attack, whatever did it would probably have come from the trees in the backyard. I didn't want Bevlov to see me lurking around there, so I grabbed a headlamp and flashlight from the cargo area and headed to the entrance of the cul-de-sac, wishing I weren't wearing heels. After turning left, I walked halfway down the block and made another left onto the footpath that ran behind the houses.

Chavez Ravine was full of hidden paths and charming little bridges spanning gullies and washes. Residents used them as shortcuts between streets and to get to the running trail bordering Elysian Park.

Bevlov's officers would eventually discover it, but there was nothing to keep me from taking a look first.

I crept along the path, searching for signs of an entity emergence. Our new heatmap was the best money could buy, and it hadn't detected anything, but I wasn't taking any chances. Entities mostly popped out of the ground without warning, pushing up through dirt and vegetation, leaving a signature hole. But nothing I found suggested an entity had broken through.

I followed the path until I could hear the hushed voices of officers on the other side of the hedge in Misty Denner's backyard.

My headlamp cut through the darkness while I navigated the twists and turns of La Loma, broadening my search along the maze of walkways. The night air was warm, but I still wished I had my trench coat. I felt out of uniform without it. And my feet were beginning to ache. Heels on dirt trails were a terrible idea.

When I reached a fork in the path, I stopped, considering which direction to take. One route led up toward Elysian Park, but I decided against it. We had security cameras along the perimeter and could check those later for any signs of activity. The other way led to Phantom's Pass via a gully that snaked through Palo Verde, eventually ending in Bishop. Some supernatural nasties had used it before to move around the neighborhoods. Before my protection spell, of course.

My curiosity pulled me toward the gully. I spent a few minutes walking up the hill, my flashlight dancing over the gnarled trees and tangled undergrowth.

Nothing but darkness and the harmless sounds of nighttime critters.

After fifteen minutes and at least two blisters, it was time to give up. I was just turning around when I saw something darting through the trees.

Something with a face of nightmares.

Chapter 3

My heart hammered in my chest. I squinted at the figure in the gully below, trying to make it out. Dark clothes. A hoodie. A face so pale it seemed to glow in the beam of my headlamp.

It didn't move, just stood there at the edge, almost blending in with the shadows, its eyes cast down.

What the hell was it? It had a human form. But many entities did, like ghouls. Of course, a ghoul wouldn't just stand there. It would shift shapes and disappear or come at me with its jaws wide open.

My mind raced while I tried to remember the emergency protocols for unknown entities. *Stay calm. Do not engage. Retreat slowly and report back to the command center.* I didn't have my slingshot, a Smoke Bomb, a baton, or even one of the pouches I had made to subdue some Chupacabras a few weeks before. In other words, I was defenseless.

When I took a step back, the figure in the gully turned its eyes toward me. They gleamed like black stones. The skin on its face was all wrong, white and ragged, like a hundred bits of torn paper glued together.

I had the sudden impression he was wearing special effects makeup, like they used in horror movies. It was sinister and ugly as hell.

It could have been a new type of entity, one that hadn't been identified by Occult Affairs yet. If that was what it was, it had been able to get through my anti-entity spell around Chavez

Ravine. It could also have been what researchers feared might one day appear: an entity 2.0, Darker and deadlier.

Something about it tugged at the edges of my memory.

I should have been afraid. But this was *my* turf, my territory. And whatever it was, it didn't belong here. I might not have been armed with my usual arsenal, but I had something else—magic. A little bit, anyway. I had used it before to get myself out of a tough spot, and I could use it again.

Hopefully.

"Hey," I called into the darkness. "Chavez Ravine Security. Get up here and show yourself."

The dark eyes blinked in the beam of my headlamp.

"You heard me," I said. "Backup is on the way. They'll be here in seconds."

I hadn't really expected the man—or whatever it was—to scramble up the embankment. He just needed to know who was in charge.

I guess he got the message. He ran.

Which was better than attacking me but meant I needed to run after him. In heels. On a dirt path. With blisters.

Off I went.

He moved in a disjointed way, as though he were in pain. I was closing in and could have caught up with him, except I slipped on the dark trail, rolled an ankle, and landed hard on my knees, howling in pain and frustration.

When I pushed myself up, my headlamp caught the figure in the gully below. He paused for a moment and glanced up at me with those unnerving black eyes.

Slowly, he turned and began to walk away, as though he didn't have a care in the world.

There was a defiance in his stride that just pissed me off.

My hands grew hot and itchy. I whipped off my right heel, and a surge of heat coursed through my body. The heel glowed with a faint purple light, which surprised and reassured me.

I wound up and hurled the shoe down at the figure below. My improvised weapon traveled quickly and surely. It seemed to accelerate while it flew through branches, not touching a single one, and smashed into his head. He staggered, then broke into his stumbling run.

"I'm going to find you," I shouted after him.

Hands clenched, I watched him disappear into the darkness of the gully.

I fished my phone out of my purse and called Ron.

"I need you to get back to the command center and watch the cameras very closely. You're looking for a man. Dark clothing, pale skin, walks with a limp or like he's in pain. He's in the gully now, but he could walk out to a street at any time, or he could keep going all the way to Phantom's Pass. If you see him, note every detail you can. If we're lucky, he'll get into a car, and you can get the plates."

"You got it, boss."

"Thanks, Ron. I know this is another late night for you, and I appreciate it."

I stuffed the phone into my purse, wiped the gravel from my bloody knees, and tried to look as dignified as a forty-year-old woman wearing one shoe and a dirty party dress could. Then I hobbled back down the path to the crime scene.

Chapter 4

A phone call would have been nice. Or even a message.

Of course, neither was required. It just would have been a matter of professional courtesy, a little heads-up that Leesa Bevlov had called a press conference for the next morning.

But no. I found out by seeing it on the news, just like everyone else.

The timing was astonishing. Autopsies weren't typically done so fast, so someone had used their clout to push Misty to the front of the line. Maybe because she was rushing things, Bevlov didn't have a lot to say about Misty Denner. Just that she was fifty-one, her death had been ruled a homicide, the cause of death was a broken neck, and the assailant had gained entry through an open bedroom window. No mention of bitemarks or foul odors.

Bevlov, wearing a drab brown jacket and too much lipliner, ended with the standard plea to the public. "We urge anyone who may have seen or heard anything unusual to come forward. Even the smallest detail could be significant. If you have any information, please contact our tip line."

Then Bevlov shared Denner's address in La Loma. The HOA board was not going to like that.

I scheduled a staff meeting for later in the morning and notified my team.

While my guards later searched Phantom's Pass and the gully, looking for evidence of activity—entity or otherwise—news of Denner's violent end began to make its way onto various Hollywood news sites, complete with an obituary.

The murder led the local TV newscasts, with live reports from outside the La Loma guardhouse.

I was watching the story when a police car crawled slowly behind the reporter and toward the guardhouse. As a private gated community, we had the luxury of keeping out pesky reporters, but now that murder had arrived in Chavez Ravine, the police department could come and go as it wished.

Uniformed officers were already going door-to-door in Misty's neighborhood, conducting interviews and collecting information. Most people were at work, so I doubted they found out much, but it was certainly a new experience for our residents.

I monitored the news and social media from my office at Palo Verde Plaza. My friend and former colleague from Occult Affairs, Jo, called from the unit's command center to check in.

"You can't catch a break up there," Jo said. "And before you ask, I checked the logs. No entity eruptions around Chavez Ravine last night."

I stopped scrolling through the nighttime surveillance video from our cameras near Elysian Park. "We have a heatmap too, remember? And nothing on ours either."

"Mads, I'm curious. We've always talked about the possibility of entities 2.0, right? A new kind of entity that shows up, alert and pissed off, not knowing where they are and not smart enough to seek shelter? So, La Loma is next to Elysian Park, and if a new version of entities appears, what's to stop them from heading into your neighborhood?" She paused. "Did you get a chance to look around the scene before we showed up?"

"Between you and me, yeah, I was there," I said vaguely.

Jo snorted. "Well? Tell me. Did it look like the work of an entity?"

"Maybe? I don't know. A ghoul possibly? Except if it were a ghoul, I don't think we'd have much of Misty Denner left. And I don't think an ogre could have squeezed in through that open window."

"Maybe we are dealing with something new, then."

"Jo, is there something you're not telling me? Are you guys seeing new entity types?"

Jo sighed. "Of course not. I'd tell you. We're still on the same side. What does Stu say?"

Stu was head of a private security firm that catered to famous clients. He also happened to be my boyfriend, which was a silly word for people our age. "Boyfriend" should have been retired long before one hit forty. Although "gentleman friend" sounded like something out of Jane Austen, and "partner" suggested things were happening that weren't. Yet.

"We haven't had a chance to talk, but he was nervous enough that he sent Clare back to her mom's. He's been working crazy hours and didn't want her to be home alone."

Stu lived in Palo Verde, the neighborhood just west of La Loma. His teenage daughter, Clare, had a troubled relationship with her mother, probably because the woman had cheated on Stu with Clare's best friend's father.

"I bet your neighbors are freaking out," Jo mused.

She was right about that. Murders were shocking anywhere, but even more so in Chavez Ravine. That sort of thing might have happened down in Los Angeles, but not here. Julia was rattled. Leo, the prosecutor for the DA's office who lived next door with his chef husband, had said he felt as if his "refuge and sanctuary" had been violated. Then he asked me to join them for G&Ts that evening, so the infringement wasn't serious enough to put a damper on his cocktail hour.

I had suspected Leo wanted to pump me for information, so I made an excuse about working late.

Jo and I ended our call with a pledge to share information, but I didn't tell her about Pale Limping Guy. If I had, she would have been obligated to pass it on to Bevlov, and Bevlov would know I was snooping around against her orders.

I went back to the surveillance video.

Near the end, I noticed a figure darting across the running trail, but when I rewound it, it was just a coyote.

I made a copy of the video from all our cameras in the hours leading up to the attack. Bevlov would eventually want it. If she had been nicer, I would have sent it over, but as things stood, I was going to make her ask.

My phone rang again. Becca Tey was livid about her interview with Bevlov. Apparently, it wasn't just me—the woman was an equal opportunity jerk.

"First, I'd already talked to her partner, but she wanted to talk to me too. Then she made me wait forever because she was talking to the medical examiner. Then she practically threatened me not to say anything about those bitemarks. I think she's afraid I'm going to sell the information to a tabloid or something. Like I'd ever help those assholes."

I mentally kicked myself for not inspecting the wounds more closely when I'd had the chance. "Did Bevlov say anything about the bites?"

"No. I did ask, but she was cagey. She just kept repeating that, for the sake of the investigation, I needed to keep it to myself. She was very pushy. I wouldn't say anything anyway, but I hate being treated like that. They can't legally stop me from talking, right?"

"Not without a court order, but that takes time, so she must have figured bullying you was the next best thing."

"Well, that's *two* reasons I don't like her. The first being her heinous dye job." Becca sniffed. "I just wish you were handling things, and I told her so."

I'm sure Bevlov loved that.

Honestly, I didn't know if I *was* capable of "handling things." When I first entered the house, I had been too focused on the strange odor to check for footprints or notice the shape and depth of the bitemarks. I knew better, but I was rattled.

"Becca, I need to run. I've got a staff meeting in a few minutes, and I need to get ready."

That meant a run to Muertos Café for some pan dulce. My team was going to need some morale-boosting. We'd had a murder on our turf, and an outside agency had swooped in and taken control of the case. It was the natural order of things, but still. My guards had recently battled some nasty entities that had broken through a protection spell, and they had been heralded as heroes. But now, with Bevlov in charge, they would face daily reminders they were just security guards working for an HOA.

When I walked into Muertos, it was as busy as ever. The lunch service was over, and the tables were crowded with people sipping espresso drinks and talking in low, worried tones about the Misty Denner case.

As soon as I had placed my order, a woman with a sharp, blunt haircut tapped my shoulder. "Why in the world didn't we get an alert about that horrible, horrible murder in La Loma last night? Why did we have to hear about it on the news?"

Heads turned in our direction.

Though I wasn't a celebrity exactly, people knew who I was, thanks to the Bad Pete viral video. I probably should have kept my head down until I'd had a chance to meet with the HOA board and decide on how best to handle worried residents.

"It was a homicide, ma'am, so it's a police matter." I kept my voice pleasant but firm. It wasn't a great answer, I admit, but I hoped it would buy me time to get my order and get out of there.

It didn't.

An older man with silver hair and a dark mustache shook his head. "Doesn't matter. We should have heard about it before the rest of Los Angeles. We live here. We have a right to be warned if there's a killer on the loose. Our windows were open last night. If we'd have known what happened, we would have locked 'em up."

Ms. Blunt Cut bobbed her head up and down in agreement. "That's right. Even if it's a police matter, you're in charge of security, aren't you? What are we paying all those dues for if we can't get basic information about a murder in our own backyard!"

Murmurs of agreement rippled through the café. The woman wasn't wrong, but there was no good way to explain why the board had decided not to send an alert. Because I didn't understand it either.

"The board is holding an emergency session, and I'm sure alerts will be on the agenda," I answered briskly. I flashed what I hoped was a dazzling smile, grabbed my order, and dashed out.

Chapter 5

Back at Palo Verde Plaza, I went straight to the command center, where my team was just starting to gather.

Bailey Nixon plopped down in a chair and began fanning herself with her hand. I had worked with Bailey in Occult Affairs, and when I needed to bring on more staff, she had been one of my first hires.

She eyed the pink box in my hands. "Is that for us? I could definitely use some sugar right now."

I smiled. "You know it is. Help yourself."

"You don't have to tell me twice."

Bailey's long copper hair was tied up in a ponytail. Despite the heat of the day, the yellow eyeshadow ringing her brown eyes hadn't smudged a bit.

She followed me to a table, where I placed the pastries, paper plates, and napkins. Bailey peered inside the box before reaching for a chocolate concha.

She was an avid runner and gym rat who could pound down a ton of food without gaining an ounce. Also helpful, she was under thirty.

Ron Mendez was sitting at the heatmap console, staring moodily at the giant screen on the opposite wall.

"Nothing, nothing, and more nothing," he said. "I'm seriously considering going back to the guardhouse. What's the point of me sitting here all day if we're never going to have another entity emergence?"

Bailey kicked the back of his chair. "You can't know that. Get a grip."

"Maybe I *do* know that." Ron cast a sly look in my direction. His family had deep roots in Chavez Ravine, and he was familiar with the supernatural parts of its history. He also knew I had brujería—Mexican witchcraft—in my family.

I hadn't told Ron I had created a protection spell over Chavez Ravine to ward off entities, but I was sure he had figured it out. And unlike me, he seemed sure it would last forever.

In the meantime, we had the heatmap, which helped the community sleep at night and was an important tool in case Ron's confidence turned out to be misplaced.

I really didn't want my questionable magical skills to become a topic of conversation, so I shot Ron a look that said, "Don't say another word." He shrugged, served himself a piece of pan dulce, and began chatting with Liam Hansen, a hulk of a guy and another former Occult Affairs officer. Liam's yellow hair was plastered to his sweaty head.

Justin Torres was the last to arrive. "Sorry, boss," he said. "My wife was freaking out about that murder, so I had to swing by and calm her nerves."

Justin lived in a nice condo with his wife and baby, a luxury they could not have afforded without discounted housing—a perk for employees of the Chavez Ravine HOA.

When Justin took his seat, I stood up and scanned the faces of my young team. Their expressions were guarded. They exchanged quick glances with one another but avoided my gaze, waiting for me to address the elephant in the room.

I cleared my throat. "Okay. Let's talk about last night. But first, everything I'm about to say stays in this room. Got it?"

When there were nods all around, I continued.

"Apparently, some residents are wondering why I didn't send out an alert after we discovered the body. Well, this is going to sound like a technicality, but the board is not legally required to notify the community about criminal activity. This isn't a blame game, but it's the board's decision to send an alert unless there is an immediate threat, like there was with the Chupacabras. They decided not to send one in this case, and we need to respect that decision. Alerts can have unintended consequences, so I must defer to the board. And just a reminder that when we all lived down in LA, we never got alerts about violent crimes, even if they happened next door. We found out on social media or TV, just like everyone else."

Their expressions relaxed a bit.

"Next, Detective Leesa Bevlov has made it clear she and the LAPD are in charge, and, to put in bluntly, I got some strong back-off vibes."

Ron held up his hand. "We got those too, boss. She wasn't too happy when she found out we'd talked to the neighbors."

"She wasn't too happy I went into the house either." Brandon brushed pink crumbs from the front of his shirt.

Bailey snorted. "Sounds like Bevlov. I worked with her a couple times, when the chief loaned me out to homicide because they were short-staffed. She's such a hard-ass."

"My buddies over there call her Leesa Blahblah because she loves to lecture people." Justin smirked.

Liam threw his head back and laughed. "I heard that too!"

I allowed myself a moment of satisfaction. Catty maybe, but I had earned it.

"Look, Brandon, I'm not sure what else you were supposed to do. You had to see if the poor woman was alive and needed medical attention. I'll have your back if things get ugly."

Brandon and Ron exchanged nervous glances, then Ron spoke up. "She asked if you'd gone into the house and—"

Brandon interrupted, his voice rising. "We said you didn't. We knew she'd tear into you. When I was hanging out with Becca Tey, she said she didn't plan on saying anything either. Did she?"

"No," I replied, cringing. Now everyone on my team knew I had entered the crime scene. "Let's just be careful. We have to do our jobs, but if we get Bevlov riled up, she can make things difficult for us. So, be discreet, okay?"

Nods all around.

"All right. Let's talk about what we know. Did anyone see anything in Phantom's Pass or the gully?"

Bailey shook her head. "Not a thing, and we walked it from one end to the other. Honestly, the brush is so dense in places that it's possible we missed something, but I don't think so." She paused. "Brandon said the victim was covered in bitemarks, but Bevlov didn't mention it in her presser. Is there any way we can find out what the medical examiner thinks caused them? I doubt Miss High and Mighty will share that information with us minions."

My neck was beginning to tighten. "If anyone has a buddy in the ME's office, now's the time to say so."

Justin, Liam, and Bailey exchanged looks and gave a collective sigh.

"What did those bites look like to you?" Justin asked.

I shuddered thinking about the horrible wounds. "It's really hard to say. I only had a quick look. They could have been made by a person or by a large animal of some kind." I paused. "And here's something else. I smelled a foul odor when I went inside—"

Brandon whipped his head toward me. "You smelled it too? Aww, man, I thought I'd imagined it."

26

"It was pretty overpowering. And disgusting. For the rest of you, it smelled like wet, dirty dog mixed with body odor and maybe a helping of rotting meat. Everyone who entered that house had to have smelled it, and they'll be wondering about it too."

I walked over to the table and took a concha and a napkin.

"One more thing. I was poking around in the gully behind the Denner place last night, and I saw what looked like a man wearing dark clothing. His face was pale and he had trouble moving, like he had a limp or some kind of injury. He saw me and took off toward Bishop, so keep an eye out. Ron, I assume he didn't do a cameo for any of our cameras?"

"No, nothing."

Justin finished demolishing a second pastry and wiped a napkin across his wide mouth. "So, what's the plan?"

That was a million-dollar question, and all I had was a two-dollar answer. Only three members of my team had police training, and Bevlov didn't want us involved in her investigation in any way. But nobody in that room was going to be happy standing on the sidelines when they had a community to protect. There was still a lot we could do. We just had to be careful to do it under the radar.

"We may be getting ahead of ourselves," I said, "but there are two things we know about Misty: she was female, and she lived alone. If our killer decides he's—*it's*— in the mood to strike again, it may target a similar victim. Let's come up with a list of women living alone. We don't want to alarm anyone, but it wouldn't hurt to add an extra patrol or two after dark."

Liam raised one of his giant hands. "There's a third thing. About Misty. She was a scream queen back in the day. Not so much lately—like thirty years ago or something. But she still gets lots of parts in horror movies." His rough skin reddened. "I'm

27

big into horror. One of the obits said she was making a monster movie at the studio next to Bishop. Sounds kinda cool. The flick's called *Phantom's Pass*." His eyes widened. "I can't believe I didn't make the connection. I wonder if that's a coincidence or what?"

I found Liam's news fascinating. It was a thread I badly wanted to pull, and I knew exactly where to start.

But first, I had an HOA meeting to get to.

Lucky me.

I asked Liam and Justin to do some digging into Misty Denner—carefully so Bevlov didn't find out—then requested for Bailey to work on that list of women living alone in Chavez Ravine. And I let everyone know we were beefing up the command center staffing overnight. The more eyes on our cameras, the better.

With the meeting over, I pulled on my electric-blue trench coat. A nice power color to get me through the next couple of hours.

Chapter 6

The HOA boardroom was comfortable and tasteful, filled with natural light and a beautiful, dark wood table. But I knew not to let my guard down in that room. I had been burned sitting at that table before, and this time, I was prepared for whatever might be slung my way.

All the board members were there, including Hernan Frias. Most people thought of him as a retired professor of mystical studies, but I had discovered he was also a brujo. One who kept his magical abilities under wraps and who was resentful about my family and our magical heritage.

As board president, Cora Bernal sat at the head of the table, impeccably dressed in a magenta blouse, not a silver hair out of place. Charlie Perez, a real estate investor who had taken my side in the past, resembled a bulldog, with his big square head and droopy features. He wore a lime-green polo shirt. Dan Berman, a retired music executive, sipped an iced coffee and ignored me, scrolling through his phone.

And then there was Eileen Simpson, successful real estate agent and giant pain in my butt. If there were a massive earthquake, she would find a way to blame me. She began tapping her French-tipped nails on the table the moment I walked into the room.

Eileen was in her late forties, with blond hair recently cut into a shag with wispy bangs—an edgy look for someone who specialized in luxury properties. No surprise, she was the first to speak, interrupting Cora when she called the meeting to order.

"I just do not, *do not* understand how something so horrible and vile could have happened in our community. How did a murderer get around our expensive private security force? A security force we recently expanded!"

Hernan brought a hand down on the table. "And now we have the police here! In Chavez Ravine! This is an outrage."

I sat back in my leather chair with a sigh and looked over at Dan. "Your turn."

He cleared his throat. Dan had long, scraggly gray hair. He looked like he should have been wearing tie-dye and smoking weed, not sitting on an HOA board.

"Well, I am disappointed and, like Eileen, confused about how all the extra security precautions we have approved—at great expense—failed to prevent a murder. We live in a gated community, for crying out loud! The attacker cannot possibly be one of our residents, so they must have come in past the guardhouses or scaled the fence, right in front of our new cameras, or—"

"They came in from Elysian Park, obviously!" Eileen nearly shouted. "What's taking so long for that new fence to go up?"

I pressed my hands into my thighs under the table but kept my cool.

"The new fence is on schedule. It's a wall, actually, made of stone, which was the board's choice, so it takes longer to build. Everyone in this room knew the timetable when we signed the contract. And my team was expanded to handle an entity invasion, which they did very well, as you'll recall. We had no serious injuries and very little property damage, which is amazing considering we were dealing with the worst entities there are— Chupacabras and ghouls. I'm quite proud of my team, and frankly, I'm glad they're not here to listen to these attacks."

Take that, Eileen.

"I also find it interesting you assume the killer is an outsider. Why are you so certain it's not someone who lives here?"

I had to admit, I was doing much better than the last time I had faced Eileen and Hernan in that room.

Eileen frowned, but she lowered the volume. "What are the police telling you? What are they doing to catch the madman who did this to Misty?" A tendon in Eileen's neck bulged out. She wasn't just angry; she was frightened. Like Misty Denner, Eileen lived alone. Mostly. Her whiny, entitled son went to a fancy private college in Los Angeles and spent most nights at his apartment near the campus.

"The police are investigating," I replied. "I don't know anything more than you do because they are not obligated to share information with us."

Cora cleared her throat. "Don't you know the detective from your time with the department? Maybe if you asked, she would be willing to keep a former colleague in the loop."

My face grew hot. *If only she knew.*

"Unfortunately, our paths didn't cross much. And detectives are notoriously tight-lipped about their cases."

Hernan threw up his hands. "But why did you call them in the first place? That wasn't up to you."

"Señor Frias," I said, "it *was* up to me. I'm not crazy about them being here either, but I am obligated to notify the police when I discover a suspicious death."

Cora stepped in. "She's right, Hernan. We wouldn't want the association to be accused of interfering with a murder investigation, now, would we? Imagine the potential liability!"

Frias crossed his arms in front of his chest, his lips curling into a snarl. For a seventy-seven-year-old man who had battled cancer and suffered a heart attack *and* a stroke, he was feisty. And dapper too. Hernan was sporting a black sweater vest over a starched white shirt despite the heat.

"Fine." Eileen gripped the edge of the table, her knuckles white. "But what are you doing to make sure that crazy person doesn't come back? That's what I'd like to know."

I took a deep breath. "Technically, that's the LAPD's job now. But there's still a lot we can do." I explained about the extra patrols for homes with women living alone and beefed-up command center staffing.

Eileen shot her bejeweled hand in the air. "That's me. *I'm* a woman living alone. Just make sure I'm on that list." She scribbled her address on a pad of paper, tore off the sheet, and slid it across the table.

"Is that it?" Hernan demanded. "Drive a security car around? That's all you're going to do?"

Before I could reply, my phone erupted with the ring tone I had set for calls from the command center. My heart rattled around in my chest while a dozen possibilities flashed through my mind.

Another murder. Another entity sighting.

Or something worse.

I snatched up the phone and dashed out of the room.

Chapter 7

I picked up the call while I ran down the stairs and out the door of the community center.

"Ron, what is it?"

"Boss, you're not going to believe this." He could not hide his excitement about something finally happening on his shift.

I didn't share his enthusiasm. "Try me."

"I just got a call from a resident in La Loma. She said she was in the kitchen and saw something on the hillside behind her house. Guess what it was?"

I began pacing in a circle. "I am *not* in a guessing game mood, Ron."

"Sorry, boss. Basically, the way she described it, it was Dog Face Bride."

I stopped. "Do you have people on the way?"

"Yes, boss. Bailey, Justin, and Liam are headed out."

Despite the heat, I went cold all over. "How far is this sighting from Misty Denner's house?"

"Checking," Ron murmured.

I imagined him squinting at the large wall screen that showed every street and building in Chavez Ravine.

"Not far. Four blocks. It looks like one of the trails cuts through, so it would be even shorter on foot."

And easier for a person—or thing—to avoid attracting attention on the streets.

"Are you thinking Dog Face Bride could be our perp?"

"I don't know," I admitted. "But at this point, it's possible. We can't afford to rule anything out. Send me the address. And Ron—we're a security team. We don't really deal with perps."

My phone chimed with the address, but I wasn't going alone. I stormed back into the building, determined to drag Hernan Frias out of the board meeting. But, as luck would have it, he was just leaving the men's room on the lower floor.

"Señor Frias, you and I are going to take a drive. There's been a sighting of one of your pet projects in La Loma."

A heavily veined hand fluttered to his heart. "Me? Why should I go? Security is *your* job, not mine." The man had the nerve to sound indignant.

I took a hold of his elbow and gave it a little shake. "Because, Señor Frias, you conjured up some really nasty creatures—"

"Which you destroyed," Hernan hissed.

"Have you forgotten? Dog Face Bride is still unaccounted for. Which makes this as much your problem as mine. And, may I remind you, it's in your best interest to get rid of her before she gets bolder or hungrier and more people spot her roaming around. You and I know she's not an entity, but the residents don't know that, and the board doesn't need another panic, does it?"

Hernan's dark eyes were as round as saucers. "Of course not. You don't think that she…that poor lady…"

"Do I think Dog Face Bride killed Misty Denner?" There was no way I was going to tell him about the bitemarks, but I figured a little guilt couldn't hurt. "I'll be honest, Hernan. I think it's possible. Of course, that would put you in an awkward position."

"I just don't see what I can do." For once, Hernan seemed genuinely concerned.

I steered him out the door and toward my Jeep. "Here's your chance to put those brujo skills you brag about to good use."

While we sped toward La Loma, Hernan gripped the chicken strap with one hand and placed the other on the dashboard, muttering every time I took a turn.

"Calm down. I'm not going that fast."

"Too fast for me," he snapped. "You're going to kill us before we even get there."

The man really liked his drama.

When we arrived, I parked next to Bailey's white SUV. My team was searching the neighborhood for the tall creature with a dog's head and a tattered white dress. I had encountered her once in my backyard, and I wasn't too eager to see her again. Neither was my companion, who was cowering in the passenger seat.

"I never imagined anything like this could happen," he said quietly. "This is all too much for me."

Was he trying to play the victim?

"Señor Frias, you made those things *specifically* to terrify non-Latino residents. What did you think would happen?"

Hernan huffed loudly. "That's right. That's what I wanted to do, and I'm not ashamed to admit it. We've got too many outsiders living here. If those damn city politicians hadn't tried to destroy our community all those years ago, we would have ended up a mostly Latino neighborhood. That's what I want us to be. But no. There are still families who haven't been able to return, and we have no room for them! It's just not right."

Relitigating the past was Hernan's default, but I needed him in the present.

"Hernan. One of your creations is running around loose, and you need to put it out of commission before it does any more harm." I climbed out of the Jeep. "You stay here. Keep the windows closed, in case your freaky dog shows up, wanting a word with her master."

"Where are you going?" Hernan's voice rose.

"I'm going to find my team and see if they've had any luck."

Dog Face Bride presented a big challenge. She was a supernatural creature that had been made by Hernan, an erratic brujo whose magic was even more unpredictable than mine.

I still hadn't figured out the extent of my abilities. With the help of my great aunt, Lencha Bantacorte, I had made pouches my team used to subdue a bunch of entities terrorizing Chavez Ravine, but they didn't work on the bride. Neither did the slingshots we used to take out Hernan's other creatures.

In other words, Dog Face Bride was her own thing.

From my right, I heard voices. I ran between two enormous houses, where I found Bailey, Liam, and Justin on a bridge, aiming their slingshots at the heavily wooded ravine below.

"We have her cornered. We might have caught her, but a neighbor decided to come over and complain about the noise," Bailey shouted. "Distracted us just long enough, and the bride ditched us."

I peered over the edge and caught a glimpse of movement among the brush. It was Dog Face Bride, all right, her canine features twisted into a snarl, tattered gown catching on branches while she prowled, searching for a way out.

"Did you hit her?" I asked.

Liam took aim and fired another round. "Don't know. For sure, we got close, but that thing is fast. And smart."

I nodded, considering our options. "I've got someone in the car who might be able to help. Do you think you can keep it there a little while longer?"

Justin patted a small bag dangling from his belt. "We've got a lot of ammo. Unless that thing can fly, I think we can keep her from moving too far."

Minutes later I was back, with Hernan Frias in tow.

Hernan paled when he saw her. "She's bigger than I remember." He took a step back and stared at his feet. "What do you want me to do?"

I wriggled my fingers in the air. "You conjured her. Un-conjure her!"

"It doesn't work like that." Hernan eyed the creature warily.

"A little effort wouldn't kill you."

Unfortunately, he took that as a hint.

Hernan pressed both hands against his chest, then said in a quiet, weak voice, "As a matter of fact, I'm not feeling so good. All this commotion is getting to me. I need to go home."

The creature let out a shrill howl, which set Hernan's body twitching. Mine too, for that matter.

With a thud, Dog Face Bride dropped to all fours and went crashing through the brush.

"The gully connects to Phantom's Pass," Bailey shouted.

Within seconds, all three were chasing after the creature.

I gave Frias what I hoped was a seething look of disgust. "Coward."

My team's voices grew fainter while they pursued Dog Face Bride toward Phantom's Pass. If they didn't catch it soon, it would disappear into the wilderness of Elysian Park.

On the way back to the Jeep, I had a quick word with the homeowner who had called us about the creature. I thanked her for her vigilance and assured her what she had seen wasn't an entity because the heatmap hadn't detected any. My answer didn't completely satisfy her, but she seemed pleased to get some attention.

"With a murder practically next door and now this, sometimes, I wonder what's happening to our nice, quiet neighborhood."

While I led Frias by his elbow back to my SUV, I wondered the same thing myself.

Chapter 8

Back in the Jeep, far from Dog Face Bride, Hernan Frias made a remarkable recovery.

"Can we stop at Muertos Café for some lunch?" he asked after buckling his seatbelt. "I can use a little pick-me-up after all the excitement."

Excitement? The man hadn't done a thing.

I had no intention of spending a minute longer than necessary with Hernan, but then my stomach rumbled. And it *was* Muertos. "All right. We'll stop, but we can't stay long."

"I'll eat fast." He actually managed to sound contrite.

Muertos Café was famous for its Mexican pastries, but it served delicious lunches too, and it was just around the corner at La Loma Plaza.

At the counter, I ordered a salad topped with Tajin-spiced prawns and cheesy croutons while Hernan chose chicken soup.

"Caldo?" I asked. "In this heat?"

Hernan bristled. "We Mexicans have caldo all year round, no matter the weather."

"Hello…My family is Mexican too," I reminded him.

"If you say so."

"You really are unbelievable, you know that?"

We found a table on the shaded patio. He picked up his spoon and stared down at his plate, frowning.

The soup looked and smelled delicious, loaded with fresh vegetables and a sprinkling of chopped cilantro. I was beginning to wish I had ordered it.

"Is something wrong?"

"They forgot my tortillas." Hernan eyed me innocently, like a five-year-old hoping for a cookie.

"Seriously?" I glared at him.

He stared back.

I caved.

When I pushed back from the table, the chair legs scraped against the tile floor.

"Corn, not flour," he called after me. "And make sure they're warm."

I returned carrying the tortillas in a jaunty red and yellow pouch, dropped it on the table, and started shoveling down my salad.

After a few minutes of silence, Hernan cleared his throat. "I can't stop thinking of that poor actress." His voice was barely above a whisper. "You don't really think my creature could have done it? I never meant for them to hurt anyone. I don't understand why it's still around."

I stabbed a baby heirloom tomato with my fork. "Because we haven't been able to catch it. For whatever reason, it's smarter than the others. Hernan, you make it sound like it's somebody else's problem. It's *your* problem, and you need to take responsibility for getting rid of it. Are you sure you can't figure out how to do that?"

"I wish I could, but it's not that easy." Hernan buttered a tortilla, frowning. "Remember when I told you my magic isn't precise? It doesn't come with an off switch. It's more about making things happen…or keeping things *from* happening. I've never had to reverse anything."

I eyed his tortilla enviously. "Mind if I have one?"

Hernan clucked his tongue. "How can I deny someone a handmade tortilla?"

"Even if the someone is a Bantacorte?" I slid a warm tortilla from the pouch. It was thicker than storebought, with uneven edges—fresh off the griddle. The humble food never failed to warm my heart.

"Even if she's a Bantacorte." Hernan actually smiled.

I speared a wedge of avocado from my salad, mashed it onto the tortilla, sprinkled it with salt, and rolled it up.

I dropped Hernan off at his home in Bishop and headed for my office. When I was almost there, my phone rang. It was Bailey.

I put the call on speaker. "Did you track down Dog Face?"

"No, I wish. We searched the entire gully, but there was no sign of her. No sign of the pale guy either. We're going to keep looking, but there is something you should know. We ran into a guy with a backpack snooping around Phantom's Pass. None of us recognized him."

"A guy with a backpack on a hiking trail? That's not suspicious." I turned into the parking lot closest to my office.

"Except he didn't look like a hiker. Too…official. So, we asked who he was and what he was up to."

"And?"

"He said he's Blahblah's partner and he was having a look around."

"Yes, I've met him. Jeff something."

"That wasn't his name. It was Steve Zhao."

"That's odd. Why would Bevlov have a new partner already? Unless Jeff got sick or something?"

"He didn't say anything about that. We just had the impression he was up to something."

"Why? What was he doing?"

"Just standing there, staring at the ground."

That didn't sound like someone investigating a murder.

"Thanks for letting me know, Bailey. I'll see if I can find this mysterious Steve and introduce myself."

I drove to Bishop and cruised the road that paralleled Phantom's Pass, stopping when I spotted a newer silver sedan, the kind of bland vehicle most plain clothes detectives seemed to prefer.

After changing into hiking boots, I headed up to the gap cutting through the ridge. Somewhere on the other side lay the movie studio where Misty Denner had filmed her last performance. It had been a cruel twist of fate—her death was like something straight out of the horror movies she had made.

It took less than five minutes to find the man. He was so engrossed in his task he didn't hear me approach, so I took a moment to try to figure out what he was doing.

At first glance, I thought he was gathering evidence. But nope. Steve was inserting a cylindrical tool into the ground, with a spade and plastic bags lying at his feet. I had caught the detective collecting soil samples, which was weird for a murder detective but exactly what an Occult Affairs researcher would do.

Interesting. And infuriating.

"Excuse me," I said.

Steve's body spasmed. He quickly straightened and spun around. "Oh! I had no idea anyone was around."

Because you didn't think you'd get caught.

"I'm Maddy Madrigal, head of security. My folks said you were here, so I thought I'd introduce myself. See if you needed any help."

Steve Zhao was maybe thirty-five. Thin, but not in a fit way. Wire-rimmed glasses. Khaki pants, with a dark green polo shirt.

And he was nervous.

"I'm Steven Zhao. Steve. I'm good. Thank you. I was just doing a walk around the victim's neighborhood to familiarize myself with the area."

"Ah, I see. You know, this is Phantom's Pass. It's in Bishop. The Denner place is in La Loma. That's east of here. So, it looks like you *could* use some help after all."

He just stood there, looking at his shoes.

"My team said you're Leesa Bevlov's partner. What happened to Jeff?" I gazed pointedly at the tools on the ground.

He crossed one leg in front of the other. "Just some last-minute…reshuffling."

Oh, Steve.

"You wouldn't happen to be from Occult Affairs research, would you?"

"Me?" Steven's voice rose. "Why would you…" His words trailed off.

I pointed at the cylindrical probe. "Homicide detectives don't usually go around taking soil samples. Come on, Steve. I'd appreciate some honesty here. I'm ex-Occult Affairs myself, so let's not bother denying why you're here. Occult Affairs has been *dying* to figure out why we don't have an entity problem, and the murder has finally given the chief an excuse to sneak in a nerd."

Steve flushed. "Hey! That's not cool."

I sighed. Spoken like a true nerd.

I had an idea.

"I'll tell you what's not cool, Steve. Trespassing. And vandalism. Since you're not investigating a murder, you're guilty of both of those things. And my bosses feel very strongly about unauthorized police activity on their private property, for reasons I'm sure you understand. They'll enjoy making an example out of you."

Steve began to squirm. There was a real possibility he might pee his pants.

I shifted to my soothing voice, the one that sometimes calmed newly arrived entities. "Look, Steve. I may be able to help you out. Maybe we can come to an agreement."

"What do you mean?" His eyes were focused somewhere around my knees.

"It's simple. I'll let you continue with your soil sampling—and whatever nerdy things you need to do—if you agree to keep me in the loop on the murder investigation. Deal?"

He hesitated. His eyebrows bunched up while he considered my offer. "Fine. But only the basics, and only because it's easier than admitting I got caught. We're under strict orders not to rile the powers that be here."

That was interesting. Bevlov hadn't hesitated to provoke *me*.

Steve continued. "If you ever say anything to Detective Bevlov, I'll deny it." The way he pronounced her name gave me the distinct impression he didn't like the woman.

I raised my hands in the air. "No worries there. She and I aren't exactly chummy. This will stay between us. What's your number, in case I need to get hold of you?"

We exchanged contact information, and I turned to walk back to the Jeep.

Behind me, Steve cleared his throat. "Maddy, may I ask you a question? You don't have to answer if you don't want to, but I'd appreciate some advice."

I turned around. "Shoot." I'm a total sucker when a younger person asks for guidance.

Steve loosened up while he talked about his project. "I'm looking for the most likely entity entry points in Chavez Ravine. You know, to test them. I've studied the heatmaps, but where else should I be looking?"

I had a couple of ideas, so I rattled them off while Steve took notes on his phone.

"Thank you. My turn. So far, Blahblah…" He turned bright red. "I'm sorry. I mean Bevlov. Bevlov has no suspects yet. The bitemarks have her guys stumped. They can't figure out if they're human or entity. The medical examiner basically said she has no clue what made them, but she thinks it was humanoid."

Would Dog Face Bride qualify as humanoid? Maybe.

"What about canine? Could it have been a dog or a wolf?"

"I didn't hear anything like that." Steve wiped sweat from his brow with the back of his hand."

"Is Bevlov talking to anyone at the movie studio where Misty was filming?"

"Not that I know of, but I'm not included in a lot of stuff. She's pissed off I'm here instead of Jeff. I know she's talking to the ex-husband and a couple of guys Misty met on those dating apps for older people."

Steve crouched and began gathering his tools.

"Thanks, Steve. Let's keep talking. By the way, if you get hungry or need a coffee, you can't go wrong with Muertos Café."

He stood. A shy smile came to his face. "Cool. I'll check it out." A pause. "I heard you live here."

I nodded. "Yeah, I do."

"You're lucky. We're stuck in the Hollywood Hills. Like I don't get enough entities at work. I can't escape them at home either. I inherited the house from my parents, and I can't sell it because no one wants to live there anymore."

Steve was right; I *was* lucky. I had a great job and a nice home. Maybe eventually I'd have someone nice to share it all with.

It made dealing with all the Bevlovs and Hernans tolerable.

I walked back down the hill with a smile on my face and the sun warming my shoulders.

Chapter 9

I wasn't exactly an expert on murder, but that didn't stop Cora from calling me every ten minutes with questions about what had happened, what the police were doing, and what she should say to the board.

When I finally pulled into my driveway, it was nearly an hour later than normal, and Sam, my red Bengal, greeted me at the door with a series of scolding meows. He rarely showed me affection but often let me know he was annoyed when I was gone too long.

In other words, he was a cat.

I poured a glass of red wine, plopped myself on the wicker couch in the sunroom, and read through my emails. One was from Cora explaining that, after listening to my advice and a barrage of complaints from residents, the board would henceforth notify its members about violent crimes in Chavez Ravine.

Good move. *Safe* move.

My phone chimed. It was a text from Julia. She and her new boyfriend—Ben Tomas, Chavez Ravine's master landscaper—were on their way over.

Normally, I would have been irked by the intrusion on my first alone time of the day, but Julia and I both had older homes without central air, and Ben was coming over to install a couple of air conditioning units.

Twenty minutes later, the door banged open. Julia swept in wearing a green sundress, her auburn hair pulled high.

She bent over and kissed Sam on the head. "You must be so hot in all that fur, yeah?"

Sam would only allow two people to treat him like that. And I wasn't one of them.

He purred loudly.

Ben appeared moments later carrying a large box, which he put on the coffee table. "I'll be right back."

When he returned, he was loaded down with another.

"Ben, this is awfully nice of you. Just let me know how much I owe you."

He shook his head. "Nothing. This was Charlie Perez's idea. The board's picking up the tab. I've got a third one in the truck. I'll be back in a sec."

Charlie must have felt guilty about my beat down at the board meeting.

"Did you hear anything more about the murder?" Julia sat next to Sam and stroked his neck.

"Not really." She didn't need to know about Misty Denner's strange wounds. It would just lead to more questions than I could answer.

Ben Tomas glanced around, nodding. "It looks real nice in here."

"Thanks to Julia's good taste." I reached over and squeezed her knee.

Sam batted at my arm.

"Hey. Behave yourself, mister. That's no way to treat the hand that feeds you."

"Where do you want 'em?" Ben asked.

I thought for a moment. "Bedroom, here in the living room, and the kitchen." The rooms where I spent most of my time."

Ben fetched a ladder and toolbox from his truck and went about his work.

47

"Julia, why don't you and Ben stay for dinner?" I poured her a glass of wine.

"Ben and I were going to grab a pizza on the way home, but we could have it delivered here instead."

"Why don't you let me make you something? I've got plenty of stuff in the fridge."

Julia thought for a moment. "Fideo? I love the way you make it."

And it was an easy dish. "I have some flap steak already cooked. How about we chop it up and throw it in?"

She took a sip of her wine. "Mmm, yeah!"

I put Julia to work dicing a large white onion while I rummaged around for the package of skinny noodles. It was simply a matter of browning the fideo in olive oil, adding the onions, tomato sauce, and a few spices, and letting the whole thing simmer in chicken broth for a few minutes.

Half an hour later, the three of us were sitting at the table in my nice, cool kitchen, bottles of Mexican beer at our elbows.

Ben had just started on his second helping. "Oh my god, this is so good. My mom makes it soupy, but I like yours better. It's more like pasta."

I went to the fridge and returned with a bowl of parmesan. "Try this instead of the cotija."

Ben spooned the cheese onto his noodles. A moment later, he was nodding and smiling.

"Told you Maddy knows how to cook," Julia said. "And she has other skills too."

"Julia," I said in a warning voice.

"I've heard a few things." Ben shrugged.

The skin on my arms went all prickly. "What things are you talking about, exactly?"

Ben set down his fork. "The bruja stuff. It's not a big secret. Lencha and your grandmother, Lily, were famous. A lot of people with family from the old days think that's why you came back."

"I came back because I was offered a job." I sounded sterner than I intended.

"Sure, but I've seen all the new plants you bought for your garden. Those are used in brujería."

Ben knew his plants. And as a legacy stakeholder who could trace his family back to the beginning of Chavez Ravine, he would be aware of its history too.

"Curanderia, not brujería," I corrected. "Grandma Lily was a healer, not a witch."

Ben stood and began collecting our empty plates. "Okay. But Lencha was a straight-up bruja. I've heard the stories. Chavez Ravine was a pretty haunted place. Monsters. Ghosts. La Llorona. She had to deal with all of them. She even banished El Cucuy."

That caught my attention. My great-aunt hadn't mentioned the boogeyman in her notebooks.

Ben set the plates in the sink and continued. "Honestly, with everything happening around here, people are relieved you're around, you know. Just in case things get really bad, it's nice to have someone with skills. If you know what I mean."

Hey, no pressure. That's why I had kept my family legacy private. You know, keep expectations low. That plan wasn't working out too well.

Julia gently touched my arm. Her fingers were soft and cool on my skin. "It's nice so many people believe in you, yeah?"

"Yeah, I guess." So far, I had only tried my magic on entities. I had no idea how to tackle a human villain.

Assuming the killer *was* human.

49

Chapter 10

When my great-aunt reached beyond the grave to give me her notebooks on brujería, I had been thrilled. I was touched and amazed she had managed it, but there was still a lot I didn't know.

Lencha Bantacorte had learned her craft from her grandmother and mother on a remote ranch in Mexico. She had her own method of doing things, but like most women practicing brujería in the old days, there was no easy way of connecting with other brujas. In other words, Lencha knew what she knew, not the history or context of her craft.

I had been raised with storybook witches, so I had plenty of preconceptions—and misconceptions—about witchcraft. It was slightly disappointing there were no magic wands or boiling, bubbling cauldrons doing the heavy lifting. Real witchcraft was hard work.

I had a full-time, stressful job and a bias toward action. In other words, I wasn't exactly patient. Brujería would require time and a certain degree of focus and mindfulness, which was hard for me. I was far more comfortable crushing herbs and following Lencha's instructions.

It all seemed overwhelming, like starting a whole new life.

I needed to go for a walk.

After changing into shorts and sneakers, I headed out, cutting through one of the steep, narrow paths and ending in a little park with a pond. A woman and her two small children were leaving, so I had the place to myself.

Maybe it was my peaceful surroundings or the drone of insects, but I could sense myself relaxing. The barrage of thoughts and worries that assaulted my consciousness began to quiet.

I sat cross-legged on a grassy verge, closed my eyes, and did some deep breathing. If I was ever going to be able to focus, that was the time.

I pictured the Lencha sculpture Julia had made. The intricate folds of her dress. Her enigmatic expression. My thoughts began to drift. I needed a more detailed image.

The Occult Affairs command center popped into my head. I sighed.

Who invited that?

I tried to move it aside, to go back to Little Lencha, but the command center was stuck in my head.

To be fair, I had spent a lot of time there, chatting with Jo. I thought of the heatmap on the wall. Jo leaning forward, talking into a microphone, dispatching a crew to an entity emergence. I remembered the time a mermaid had appeared at a marina on LA's west side. Not sweet, innocent Ariel, but the not-so-nice variety with sharp teeth. Jo had sent me and two other Occult Affairs officers to pick her up.

By the time we got there, the mermaid had hauled herself onto a boat dock and was flopping around in the throes of entity confusion. We used steel mesh gloves and a net to capture her, but it had taken the better part of an hour. I could still remember the lost look in her blue eyes and the way her scales shimmered in the sun.

While I sat in the grass, I decided to stop fighting the mermaid image and instead embraced the memory. I willed my mind to keep her image clear and vivid. My hands itched, and a warm tingling sensation spread up my spine. The air around me seemed to hum.

I opened my eyes. A sense of unease washed over me. Out of the corner of my eye, I caught movement at the far end of the pond.

A small splash.

And then water rippling, as if something were moving slowly toward me, just under the surface.

My heart slammed against my chest, like it was trying to break out.

I jumped to my feet and stumbled back.

A head emerged. Long, flowing green hair, skin the color of raw cod. A wide mouth bulged, as if it were covering a mass of teeth. It was the mermaid from my memory but without the usual entity confusion.

Panicked, I shouted, "No! Go away!"

The mermaid slowly began to swim toward me. Her turquoise eyes were mesmerizing. My witchcraft practice session had gone horribly, terribly wrong.

I stomped my foot. "I said, go away!"

The green-haired creature tilted her head and blinked.

I had accidentally conjured the mermaid. But how, exactly? And what about my protection spell?

I was the head of security, responsible for keeping entities *out* of Chavez Ravine, and yet, I had just invited one in. If the board found out, I would be gone before I could say "bad bruja."

Yelling at her would get me nowhere. I needed to reverse whatever I had just done. But first, I needed to put some space between us, in case she slithered out of the water.

Just when I reached a far corner of the park, voices sounded on the path.

Shit.

I ran toward the approaching footsteps. A man carrying a little boy on his shoulders was walking up the path. I must have appeared crazy because he took a giant step back when he saw me.

"Hi. I'm Maddy Madrigal, head of security. I'm afraid we're dealing with a little situation at the park, and it's temporarily closed." I forced a reassuring smile to my face. "Nothing serious. It'll be open again tomorrow morning."

I hoped.

The child stared at me, wide-eyed.

The man had the slouchy build of someone who spent too many hours sitting behind a desk. "What *kind* of situation?" he asked.

I shook my head. "Nothing serious. But I really need to get back to it."

He looked like he was about to argue, but I gave him my best don't-you-dare look, and he turned on his heel and left.

When I got back to the pond, the mermaid was trying to crawl out of the water, flopping higher on the bank. I pushed the image of my career ending out of my mind, closed my eyes, and focused. I pictured the toothy mermaid falling back into the water and disappearing into a sinkhole at the bottom of the pond.

A splash.

Getting rid of her couldn't have been that easy, could it?

Probably not.

I cracked open one eye.

Nope. She was smiling at me, which was disgusting.

I focused all my energy on making the mermaid disappear. A wave of heat coursed through me, and the image in my head changed. The smiling mermaid was replaced by the entity's tail flicking while she moved down into a watery chasm.

The splashing stopped.

I opened my eyes.

She was gone.

I waited for what seemed like forever to be sure, almost afraid to breathe, in case she was hiding just beneath the surface, biding her time.

But no. She was really gone.

I walked away, my leg muscles weak with relief. Then I called the command center and asked Brandon to send someone to close off access to the park and check the pond once an hour until the next day. Just as a precaution.

"What should they be looking for?" Brandon asked.

That was a good question. "Not sure. I thought I saw something in the water, but I didn't get a good look. It was probably just a turtle. But you know, just in case."

"Not a problem," Brandon said.

I took deep breaths all the way home, trying to steady myself. The walk had been meant to clear my head, but I had filled it with images of a mermaid instead, and somehow one had appeared. It was impossible to say whether she had been an entity or something else. If she *was* one, that meant I had been able to bypass my own anti-entity spell surrounding Chavez Ravine.

It took the entire hike home to make sense of it all. I had managed to focus, at least for a short time, and I had made something happen. All by myself. No help from Little Lencha or my mother or a newt's eye.

Could I do that again? Under pressure? Use my magic to take out a monster or catch a killer?

Maybe I could, with more practice. The mermaid felt like a parlor trick.

The real test was still ahead.

Chapter 11

It was still early after I got home from my ill-fated trip to the park. I had time to do a little reading before hitting the sack.

The doorbell rang when I was just settling onto the couch. It was Stu. He stepped inside cautiously, watching the cat closely and holding a wine bottle, as if ready to defend himself in case Sam decided to pounce. Which made complete sense. Sam had done it before.

The cat's tail flicked in the air.

"Don't even think about it, mister," I said.

Stu edged slowly toward the living room. "You talking to me or the cat? I can't speak for Sam, but my intentions are innocent."

"That's kind of disappointing."

Stu wore faded jeans and a blue shirt that complimented his eyes. He put the bottle down on the coffee table. I couldn't help but focus on his wrists. They were strong, with a light dusting of golden hair. How the veins stood out against his tanned skin captivated me, and I couldn't seem to stop staring.

I felt a strange sensation. Either an early hot flash or a reaction—a strong one—to Stu.

He turned toward me with an uncertain smile. "Everything okay? I probably shouldn't have come over without calling first. You must be exhausted after everything that's going on. We can do this another time."

Do what?

"Don't be silly." I gestured for Stu to take a seat on the couch.

Sam prowled the perimeter of the room, seeming to take great pleasure in unnerving my guest.

I retrieved two wine glasses from the vintage cabinet I had picked up while antiquing with Julia.

"Maybe I should have brought him some treats or something," Stu said, uncorking the bottle.

"I hate to give into tyrants, but maybe a little bribery wouldn't hurt." I glanced over at Sam, who was lazily grooming himself on the windowsill, grabbed an aerator from a drawer, and handed it to Stu.

He poured the wine and put the glasses on the coffee table. The next moment, he was pulling me beside him, lips meeting mine, soft and warm. My body melted, and even though the room was cool, I was burning up.

"Wow. That was…unexpected. But nice." I leaned back on the couch and picked up my glass. From the other room, I could hear Sam batting something across the bathroom floor.

"Mmm. I'm glad I stopped by."

This was the first time in ages Stu and I had had time to ourselves, partly because his daughter was always around. "Is everything all right with Clare?"

Stu took a sip of his wine and grimaced. "She's fine, but she's pretty unhappy with me. She doesn't like staying with her mother, and she thinks I'm overreacting about the murder. But until we know more, I'm just not comfortable with her staying at my place alone." He paused. "Do *you* think I'm overreacting?"

It wasn't like Stu to second-guess himself. My thoughts drifted back to that horrible crime scene.

"Not at all. Did you know Misty Denner?"

He leaned into the cushion, keeping a warm hand on my thigh. "I never met her, but I was talking to Pete today, and he knew her. He's a big horror buff, and he met her while he was making a video at the studio next to Bishop. They got to talking, and he asked her to do a cameo. He was thrilled when she agreed. He said something else that was interesting."

"Oh?"

"Once over coffee, she said there'd been some strange incidents on the set. Small fires, stuff falling from the ceiling, and some unexplained accidents. Nothing too serious. You know she broke her ankle during filming?"

"I do. Did Pete say what Misty thought about all that? Were the filmmakers taking safety shortcuts?"

Stu shook his head. "Nothing like that. She'd worked with them before, and they were great. No complaints. But she *did* say there was a rumor something weird was going on with the film."

I sat up straight. The tension of the day came flooding back. "What? Like a poltergeist?"

"I'm not sure," Stu said grimly. "But I didn't think anything of it until now."

"Have the Hollywood trades picked that up yet?"

Stu would know. Most of his security clients were celebrities or big shots in the entertainment industry.

"Not yet. The film was mostly done, I hear, so they won't have to reshoot any scenes because of what happened." Stu leaned forward and topped off our glasses. "What are you hearing from the police?"

I snorted. "Nothing. The detective in charge of the case has made it clear she doesn't want my help."

"You're kidding? That's shortsighted, with everything you know about Chavez Ravine. I assumed they'd be all over you, trying to get the inside scoop."

I sipped my wine. Its spicy warmth slid down my throat. "Nope. And I found out the chief is trying to pull a fast one. He put an entity researcher from Occult Affairs onto the investigating team, and now the guy's taking soil samples and doing whatever else they do."

Stu frowned. "Whoa. That's ballsy. Did you file a complaint?"

"No. Better than that. I told him I wouldn't tattle if he kept me updated on the case."

Stu chuckled. "Of course you did." He leaned over and pressed his lips against my temple.

A lipstick tube shot across the floor and banged into the baseboard, causing both of us to jump. Sam stood watching us from the dimly lit hallway, his green eyes shining.

My weirdo cat always seemed to sense when something was up. Stu and I were finally alone, without Clare. We were sharing the couch, and there was nothing to stop us.

Except Sam.

Stu danced his fingers up my arm. "Do you think it's possible to lock up the cat?"

His touch set my skin on fire.

Sam meowed loudly. Sometimes, I wondered if he understood human speech.

"That's probably a good idea."

I sprang to my feet, crossed the living room, and quickly closed the hallway door. That was the easiest thing to do, but it meant the bedroom would be off-limits, unless we wanted to risk Sam taking a chunk out of Stu.

The wine had left a warm buzz in my head. Stu was on his feet, closing the distance between us, pressing me against a wall. I placed both my hands around him and pulled him even closer. He smelled good—eucalyptus and musk. My heart pounded so loudly I wondered if he could hear it.

"Are we really, finally doing this?" Stu's breath tickled my neck. His voice was low.

"Hell yes, we are, Mr. Wells," I whispered back.

In the hallway, behind the door, Sam howled.

I was glad the windows were shut and the air conditioners were running because the three of us made a lot of noise.

For two people who hadn't had sex in a long time, we managed quite well. I remembered how things worked, and Stu hadn't even come close to needing little blue pills. Either time.

Eventually, we admitted we were too old to sleep on the couch, as cozy as it was. I got up to deal with the cat. Stu, wrapped in a throw, with a pillow clutched against his private parts for good measure, shuffled to the sunroom so he wouldn't be in the direct line of fire when the cat came shooting out of the hallway.

I opened the door and rattled a bag of chicken treats. Sam circled my bare legs, meowing loudly, and followed me into the kitchen, where I fed him some nuggets and refilled his water bowl.

"Please, *please*, be nice," I implored.

From the other room, Stu called my name. "Maddy, you might want to come take a look at this." He sounded alarmed.

I hurried toward the sunroom.

Little Lencha—the figurine sculpted by Julia and inspired by my bruja great-aunt—was glowing red. It was how her spirit reached out to me, although her message wasn't always clear.

I didn't like the look of that red. It seemed like danger.

I had never mentioned Little Lencha to Stu. For that matter, I had never told him anything about my dabbling in Mexican witchcraft. It was too weird to bring up in conversation, and I had not wanted to scare him off, so I never seemed to find the right words to explain it all.

"Is this thing a lamp?" Stu ran his fingers around the figurine's base. "I can't find the switch."

I tried pulling him away, but he wouldn't budge. "The wiring is a little funky. Don't worry about it. It'll turn off on its own."

Stu frowned. The red glow intensified, casting an eerie light in the room. "Are you sure? It looks like it's about to explode or something."

"It's fine," I said lightly. "It usually does that before it goes off." I really needed to get Stu out of the room, in case Lencha did something I couldn't explain away. "Hey, there are some fresh towels in the bathroom...if you feel like taking a shower."

Stu gave the air a tentative sniff. "Wow, I think that's my cue. I'll be right back."

"Shut the door behind you. Otherwise, the cat will get in." I watched him go, enjoying the view of his well-muscled backside.

When I heard the *snick* of the latch, I turned to the figurine. "Lencha. Whatever is going on, can it *please* wait until tomorrow morning, when my gentleman friend is gone?"

Apparently, it could not.

Little Lencha pulsed an even brighter red, her clay eyes wider than I had ever seen them. I reached out and touched her shoulder. As soon as my fingers made contact, a surge of power shot through me, and a voice spoke loud and clear in my mind.

"Quidado, muchacha."

The light flickered off, and the figurine's glow faded.

My great-aunt had just warned me to be careful. But careful of what?

I was still staring at Little Lencha when Sam came over and circled my ankles, his fur brushing against my bare skin. And moments later, Stu was standing next to us, one of my bath towels hugging his hips. He smelled like my coconut shampoo.

My cat and boyfriend were now just inches apart. Stu didn't seem to notice the danger lurking at ankle level. He was too busy staring at my workbench.

"This must be what Clare was talking about." Stu slung a warm, bare arm around my waist. He nodded at the rows of ceramic bowls filled with seeds and other ingredients. A string of dried chilis hung on the wall.

"Mmm?" It didn't come out as nonchalantly as I had intended.

"Clare said Julia told her your grandmother was a witch and that you had some magic too. Or maybe it was an aunt? I can't remember."

"Both, actually. They were healers," I said firmly. "They practiced curanderia."

"Oh. Are you doing that too?"

How to explain without sounding like a nutcase?

"It's more of a hobby than anything else," I said. "More like preventative medicine."

"Like that necklace you made Clare? The one she refuses to take off?"

I nodded. "Exactly. My grandmother made cures for the women of La Loma. I didn't know much about curanderia, so I started reading up on it and decided the best way to learn about it was to actually try some of the cures."

Stu picked up a bundle of dried mint hanging from a peg and sniffed it. He nudged my shoulder with his. "This explains why you always smell so good."

"I'm not making perfume in here!" I gave him a playful nudge in the ribs. "Hey, I'm getting tired." I paused. Unexpectedly, I felt shy, and I wasn't a shy person. "Are you staying the night?"

Stu cleared his throat and looked at the cat. "Will he let me? Or will he slit my throat in my sleep?"

Sam lifted a giant paw, placed it on Stu's foot, and left it there.

My heart skipped a beat when I leaned forward to get a better look. "Are his claws out?"

"I don't think so." Stu's hand squeezed my side. "Dogs do this. The alpha male showing his dominance. I've never heard about cats doing it, though."

I sighed. "Sam isn't exactly normal."

"I can attest to that." Stu laughed but made no attempt to move his foot.

I yawned and clapped my hands. "All right, Sam. You've made your point." I flicked off the light and began walking toward the hallway.

We made it to the bedroom without Sam ripping into my sleepover guest. Stu dropped his towel and slipped under the covers. I wished I had taken a shower as well, but it was too late. There was no way I was going to leave Sam alone with poor, defenseless Stu.

Sam hopped onto the bed, settling in behind my knees. Stu grabbed my hand and kissed it. Moments later, a rhythmic breathing sounded when he fell asleep.

I wasn't so lucky. The next half hour was spent staring at the ceiling, wondering what Little Lencha had been trying to tell me.

And hoping I was up to dealing with whatever it was.

Chapter 12

If I'd had any lingering doubts about Stu, he dispelled them the next morning.

He waited until I'd had two cups of coffee before attempting conversation. If he had been a chatty morning person, I would have ended it right there.

Also, I was feeling awesome. I had forgotten how mood-altering good sex could be. In fact, I felt so good that I made chilaquiles for breakfast.

After he had taken a bite of the crunchy, savory, gooey dish, his eyes rolled back in his head. "A guy could get used to this."

"Gotta earn it every time." I ruffled his hair while I topped up his water glass.

Stu wriggled his eyebrows suggestively. "Is that your way of asking for another round?"

"If we were the hooky-playing type, I'd say yes."

He washed the dishes while I tidied the rest of the house. I found Sam in my office, sulking. It was 7:30 a.m., and he had not tried to attack Stu even once.

"Good boy," I said, trying to reinforce Sam's non-violent choices.

He gave me a disgusted look and strutted out of the room.

I was walking Stu to his SUV when my next-door neighbor, Leo, appeared on his porch. Our eyes met, and he mouthed, *Oh my God,* fanning himself.

I shot him the finger, and he laughed. Stu gave him a friendly wave, oblivious to the attention his walk of shame was attracting.

Leo's husband, Toby, appeared on the doorstep dressed in workout clothes, a mug clutched between his hands.

"Hi, Stu!" he called.

Stu waved again. I made a shooing gesture at Toby. He stuck out his tongue and retreated inside.

I gave Stu a quick kiss, suddenly self-conscious, and watched him drive away. With a sigh, I turned to go back into the house, when movement across the street caught my eye.

It was a yellow dog. Loose, no owner in sight. Even from a distance, I could tell it had a collar.

Leo slowed down when he drove past. "That's our neighbor's Lab," he called through the open window. "I think his name is Cooper."

That rang a bell. I had briefly met his owner, a young woman, when I was trying, unsuccessfully, to find Sam's. She had told me about the lost pet network in Chavez Ravine and how she had once used it to locate Cooper.

Usually by this time, I had read through all my emails and checked in with the command center, but this had not been a usual morning. I needed to get to work, but I couldn't very well allow Cooper to wander into the street.

When I crossed the road, calling out his name, Cooper stopped. His ears pricked up, and he came bounding toward me. Cooper was big and friendly. A round tag dangled from his red collar, with a phone number etched into the silver disc. I dug my phone out of my trench coat pocket, crouched next to him, and called the number while Cooper panted dog breath into my face.

No answer.

I left a message, then tapped out a text and waited a few moments.

No reply.

The dog began to whine. I had never owned a dog, but he sounded distressed. Maybe he had escaped after his owner left for work and was stuck outside. Or perhaps his owner was inside her place, having a nice, long shower, and had no idea her pooch was roaming around, loose.

The woman lived in one of eight town houses across the street, but I couldn't remember which one. She seemed to have a crazy work schedule, and on the rare occasions I did see her, she was always dressed for a run. I decided to ring doorbells until I found out where she lived.

On my second try, a wiry woman of around seventy peered through a glass panel next to the door. When she saw me with Cooper, she opened it. "May I help you?" She seemed slightly suspicious.

I was bent over, hanging onto Cooper's collar. "I'm looking for this guy's owner. Early thirties, maybe? Short dark hair?"

The woman had dyed fire-orange hair in a pixie cut. She stared at Cooper for a moment, frowning. "That would be Naomi. I caught her letting him poop in my yard once. She had a doggie bag and cleaned it up, but I think it's terrible she let him do that. I complained to the HOA, but they said since she'd done the right thing, there was nothing they could do. Those HOA people are absolutely useless." Her eyes narrowed. "Wait a minute. Aren't you that new head of security? I have a bone to pick with you."

I was sure she did, and I was equally positive I did not want to hear it. But I pasted a professional smile on my face. "My name is Maddy Madrigal. My contact information is available on the HOA's website. If you can contact me there, that would be great, but I'm late for work, and I need to get Cooper home. Can you please tell me which place is Naomi's?"

The woman pinched her lips together, stepped out on the porch, and pointed. "Two doors down. The one with the Jacaranda tree out front. Why the HOA allows those in the neighborhood, I have no idea because they make the biggest mess." She glanced down at Cooper. "I'm not surprised he's running around without a leash. She's not a very responsible owner, if you ask me."

No one asked you.

"Thank you. Sorry to disturb you. I better get going."

"Tell that girl to take care of that animal!" she called after me.

Still holding on to Cooper's collar, I steered him toward the townhouse. It was an awkward business, with me hunched over and the Lab trying to bound away, but we finally made it to the stoop. Cooper gave a hopeful bark. I rang the doorbell.

No answer.

I put my ear close to the door.

No sounds from within.

I dragged Cooper across the yard toward the gate to the back patio. It was closed, but when I pushed, it swung open. So, in we went.

I shut the gate behind us and released the dog. He ran ahead to the sliding door and began barking furiously at the glass. It was closed, but the blinds were up. I knocked.

No answer.

But Cooper seemed to think someone was inside.

I was beginning to have a not-very-good feeling.

When I knocked again, this time more forcefully, still nothing.

Something in my stomach twanged like an out-of-tune guitar. Uneasy, I glanced around. The four-piece patio set appeared new. Nothing fancy—like the stuff sold at discount warehouses—but nice enough. No potted plants or flowers hanging from baskets. There wasn't much need. The townhouses backed up onto a wooded area, so there were plenty of trees and greenery.

And places to hide.

I could bring Cooper to work with me. Drop him off at the command center until I reached the owner. Ron would be thrilled to dog-sit. But there was another, more obvious option. Cooper gave an ear-splitting yelp and bashed his head against my knee.

"All right, all right," I muttered.

The chord in my stomach rattled again. I pulled on the handle, and the glass door slid on its tracks, revealing one of those kitchen/dining room/sitting areas popular in newer construction. Everything was done in tasteful, neutral colors. A series of classic horror film posters lined one wall. No smell of coffee. A cardboard takeout container on the counter, lid raised.

I stuck my head in. "Hello? Naomi?"

Cooper pushed past me and charged inside. He seemed to know exactly where he was going. His clawed feet scraped against hard flooring. He turned a corner and bounded up the stairs.

Somewhere above my head, he came to an abrupt stop and howled.

Shit. The hair on the back of my neck lifted.

Had Naomi fallen in the shower? Smacked her head on the way down and knocked herself out?

Other nastier thoughts began to push their way in. I briefly toyed with the idea of calling Ron and asking him to send someone over, just in case. But that was ridiculous.

There was nothing amiss in the kitchen area. I crept toward the living room.

More posters from popular modern horror movies. There was a pile of books on the coffee table and another on an end table. A few empty water glasses. A bunch of unopened boxes stacked just inside the front door. No obvious footprints or signs of forced entry. All the windows were closed, the soft white blinds intact and undisturbed.

Cooper continued his frantic barking.

I moved slowly up the stairs. At the top was a short hallway and three doors, two of them closed. Cooper was standing outside one of them, his short hair raised, bristling all over. Ropey saliva dangled from his mouth.

I sniffed, and bile rushed up my throat. A foul stench filled my nostrils.

One I had smelled before.

I took a deep breath, stepped forward, pushed open the door, and peered inside. Blood whooshed in my ears, blocking out Cooper's frantic barks.

Naomi lay in a fetal position on the floor at the foot of an unmade bed. She wore an oversized black T-shirt in a print of tiny white skulls. Her arms were curled protectively around her head, and her short hair was damp.

I knelt and felt for a pulse.

Nothing.

I rose to my feet and took a closer look at the body. Jagged punctures oozing crimson droplets covered her legs.

They were just like the bitemarks I had seen on Misty Denner two nights before.

Chapter 13

I had to act fast. A call needed to be made to the LAPD, but I was determined to get a better look at the scene than I had at Misty Denner's house. Once Bevlov arrived, I would be sent back to the kids' table.

I dragged Cooper downstairs, made sure the gate was locked, and slid the door shut behind me.

While I was snapping a few pics of Naomi's wounds, I noticed the door leading into a small en suite bathroom. Using a clean tissue, I nudged it open and looked inside.

A fan whirred overhead. The only window in the room was closed. Makeup and skin care products cluttered the vanity beside the sink. The air was still warm and moist. Naomi had just finished showering when she had been attacked.

The bedroom window facing the woods stood wide open, a few blurry footprints remaining beside it, so I poked my head out and looked down at the ground. The intruder would have needed a ladder to get inside. There was no sign of one, no trellis nor drainpipe someone could have used to scale the wall.

Maybe the attacker had come in through the unlatched sliding door and gone up the stairs. Naomi could have left Cooper in the backyard while she showered. She might not have worried about anyone trying to get past him. Not with a dog that large. While not aggressive, Labs could be protective of their family and home.

The smell of wet canine and body odor was strong enough to make my eyes water. A gold-framed poster of a werewolf carrying a woman in a red dress hung above the bed. I froze, staring at the creature's menacing face.

Entities had been surfacing for a few years, but we had never encountered a werewolf. Nor zombies. Nor the kind of vampire you would expect to see in a horror flick. At least, not yet.

But what if a werewolf—or something like it—had emerged in Chavez Ravine and attacked the two women? If so, it had managed to avoid detection by the heatmap. The nerds at Occult Affairs always worried a new type of entity would eventually appear, one capable of evading the tools created to track them.

Maybe that time had come.

An ornate gold mirror hung above a black wooden desk. They both resembled props from a movie. A lanyard dangled from the mirror. I went over for a closer look.

The badge read: "Western Studios." It included Naomi's photo and her full name—Naomi Elizabeth Taylor.

That was the studio complex on the other side of Bishop, where Misty Denner had been filming when she died. Had the two women known each other?

I had been in the house long enough. It was time to go.

In the kitchen, I found Cooper's red leash hanging from a peg next to the door. All the stress and barking had left him a bit droopy. But I couldn't take him home—Cooper didn't deserve to be subjected to Sam.

I went outside and called the LAPD.

While I waited, pacing on the sidewalk under the shade of the jacaranda tree, the red-headed neighbor appeared on her porch. I dialed Ron at the command center and pressed the phone against my ear.

The neighbor didn't seem fazed in the least. "She wasn't home?"

Everyone would find out soon enough. I pretended not to have heard her. She disappeared back inside her house when Ron picked up. I explained what was going on.

"You're kidding?"

"I am not. The heatmap isn't showing anything?"

"No! Not a thing. I'd have called you." Ron sounded indignant.

Cooper collapsed at my feet, panting.

"Look, the police will be here soon, so I don't know when I'll make it to the office. The victim's name is Naomi Taylor. Get ahold of Bailey and tell her to find out whatever we can about her: how long she's lived here, name of her employer, etcetera. It looks like Naomi lived alone, so she must have been on that patrol list I asked for. I want to know when a car made the rounds because I'll be sure to get that question from the board. I'm going to call Cora Bernal and give her a heads-up."

"You got it. Do you want me to send anyone over to you?"

"No, I'm fine. Let's have Liam and Justin check out the trails behind Taylor's townhouse."

"What should I tell them to look for?" Ron asked.

"Signs of an entity emergence or anything out of the ordinary."

"I'm on it."

Twenty minutes later, several police cars rumbled up, followed by Bevlov's silver muscle car.

Bevlov's new "partner," Steve, was the first to approach. "We were delayed because an entity showed up at our last crime scene. And by that, I mean right in the *middle* of our crime scene. We had to wait for Occult Affairs to clear it out."

Steve was dressed more like a plain clothes detective and less like an Occult Affairs nerd, wearing navy blue pants and a white linen shirt. But he still looked like he worked a desk job.

"What kind of entity?"

Steve's eyes twinkled. "A nixie. The house was in Angelino Heights, a spectacular Victorian with a huge pond out back. That's where the body was discovered and where the nixie popped up. Freaked everyone out."

Nothing new, then. We had seen them before. Water entities were especially difficult to round up because Smoke Bombs didn't work in water and the entities would hide below the surface. Which meant some poor officer in a wetsuit had to wade in, hands and face covered in steel mesh, and drag them out. I thought of the mermaid I had conjured and shuddered.

Bevlov sauntered over, frowning. "So, you found the body?"

Cooper got to his feet, tail wagging, his brown eyes hopeful. The poor pooch had zero chance of getting any love out of Bevlov, but I had to admire his optimism.

"I did." Still holding onto Cooper's leash, I pointed across the street with my free hand. "I live just over there and—"

"Is this your dog? I never pegged you as a dog person."

I took a deep breath. "No. He belongs to the victim. His name is Cooper. I found him wandering around outside and decided to run him back home to keep him safe. Which is how I found…"

My voice trailed off while I took note of Leesa Bevlov's eyes, which had begun to tear up. Her mouth turned down like she was about to cry.

I stared at her, mystified. "Detective?"

Bevlov dropped to her knees and threw her arms around the dog's neck. "Oh, you poor, poor thing. You must be so confused. It's going to be okay. We're going to take good care of you."

Cooper's tail went into overdrive.

I shoved my eyeballs back into their sockets. Apparently, Bevlov saved all her empathy for creatures with four legs.

Steve appeared every bit as startled by this unexpected display. "Should I call animal control to come pick him up?"

"No!" Bevlov cried. "After everything he's been through, this beautiful animal will *not* be stuck in a pen. I'll call my husband to pick him up. We have a chocolate Lab at home. We'll keep him until we figure out the next of kin."

Steve rubbed the back of his neck. "Can we do that?"

"We can if I say we can," Bevlov said. She straightened, walked a few yards away, and began talking into her phone. She returned a few moments later. "Yuri works from home. He'll be here soon." She turned to me, and her brisk demeanor returned. "You live where, exactly?"

"I'm over there." I pointed and gave her the address.

"Wait at your place and I'll take your statement when I'm done here."

Super. Because it's not like I have anything important to do except wait for you.

Bevlov handed the leash to Steve, turned on her heel, and joined a uniformed officer, who escorted her through the gate leading to the backyard.

"What about the dog?" Steve called after her.

Bevlov spun around, scowling. "Stay with him until Yuri gets here."

"Great," Steve muttered. "Now I'm dog-sitting." He turned to me. "You have any openings?"

"That bad?"

"You have no idea." Steve gave the dog a quick pat on the head. "She's not happy they subbed me in for Jeff. She's complained to the chief, but he won't budge, so now she's trying to make my life miserable."

I patted him on the shoulder.

There was nothing to do but go home and wait for Bevlov. At least I didn't have to worry about Cooper. Bevlov would spoil him rotten.

I rubbed his neck, my fingers sinking into his fur, then headed across the street, dreading the next phone call I had to make.

Chapter 14

It was nice and cool in my house. I had no idea how long it would take Bevlov to grace me with her presence, but I didn't think she would be in a big hurry. That suited me since I needed to call Cora and give her the bad news about another murder.

Which I really didn't want to do.

I paced around the living room, put a couple of dishes away in the kitchen, and strolled into the sunroom. Anything to put off making that call.

Sam was sitting, sphinxlike, next to Little Lencha, who once again was glowing red.

I sighed. "Is that what you were trying to tell me, Lencha? That we were about to have our second murder?"

The figurine winked off, returning to her usual clay form. Communication with the spirit of my great-aunt, the famous bruja of La Loma, was inconsistent at best. My mother had said that, in life, Lencha had been a stern and taciturn woman. So why should she change in death?

I rearranged the delicate clay bowls from Julia's shop that I used to hold my supplies, but my thoughts kept drifting back to the murder scene and those terrible wounds on Naomi's soft, pale flesh.

In the kitchen, I made a pitcher of tea, added some ice cubes, and stuck it in the fridge. Then I flopped on the couch in my living room and, with a sigh, called Cora.

She answered immediately. I told her the bare minimum, leaving out the gruesome details.

"No!" she cried. "That poor girl. This can't be happening! Are you sure it wasn't an accident?"

I sighed. "Positive. And Cora, considering the reaction we got after Misty Denner's murder, we should let residents know, don't you agree?"

"Will the police allow us to do that?"

"They may not be thrilled, but there's nothing they can do to stop us, and we promised the community we would send out an alert if something serious happened again. We don't want to let them down."

Meaning, we didn't want the current board to get booted during the next election. As difficult as Hernan and Eileen were, I really didn't want to justify my job and my team to a bunch of new board members.

A swift intake of breath came through the line. Cora had gotten the message.

"Okay, then I agree. But I think it's better coming from you. You're head of security, after all, and you always know how to phrase things."

Cora was no dummy. If the police freaked out about the notification, I would be the one to get blasted, not the board. But it was a part of my job, and hiding behind Cora was not a good look.

"I'll send it now."

I went into my home office, where I fired up my laptop and wrote a carefully worded text in the HOA's communication system. My phone chimed—proof the message had gone out.

I sat back and closed my eyes, trying to push away the images of Naomi's ravaged body and the many questions her death would raise. Almost immediately, my phone blew up with calls and messages. I ignored all of them except for the one from Stu.

"Maddy," he began, sounding serious, "I have an important question for you."

Sam jumped on the desk and flopped onto the keyboard. I glared at him.

"You're not calling about the message I just sent out?"

"No, I haven't seen it yet. I've been in meetings, but I haven't been able to stop thinking about you."

My stomach did a little flip. "Oh yeah? So, what's the question?"

Stu cleared his throat. "Tonight. My place or yours?"

I nudged Sam off the keyboard. "Oh, Stu. I'd love to, but we just had a second murder, so there's no telling how late I'll be working."

When I had finished filling him in, Stu groaned. "Oh no. That's horrible." He paused. "I'm just reading your text. That's across the street from you. Wait…Did you find the body?"

"Yeah."

Stu let out a low whistle. "Damn, Maddy. Are you okay?"

The sight of Naomi's mangled body came rushing back, and a lump rose in my throat. "I'm fine. I'm just worried, that's all. I really don't want another of our residents to be hurt. But at least I found a link between the two murders. Victim number two had an ID badge for Western Studios too."

"Does the detective know that?"

"Beats me. She's not very interested in what I have to say, so she'll have to figure things out on her own." I paused. "Not to sound petty or anything."

Stu laughed. "You? Never. I'm about to call Clare and check in with her. She gets those alerts too. And just a heads-up…There's more drama on her soccer team, and she and her mom are at each other's throats. It's possible you'll hear from her. She really likes you."

"I like her too. Don't worry. I'm here with a sympathetic ear if she needs one."

When we hung up, I went back and reviewed my notifications. I returned Julia's call, then Leo's, then replied to Toby's message. Everyone was on edge, and I was frustrated I couldn't be more reassuring.

Cora called saying the board had heard from several women living alone in Chavez Ravine who demanded 24/7 protection services. "I made it perfectly clear that their requests did not fall within the HOA board's remit, but I'm going to ask if you can please follow up with them to provide whatever reassurance you can. I want them to know we're taking their security concerns seriously, and I think they'll appreciate you personally reaching out to them."

For a woman who ran a tamale empire, Cora could sound as much like a lawyer as my neighbor Leo.

We had just finished saying goodbye when there was a knock at the front door.

Actually, it was less of a knock and more of a pounding.

Bam. Bam. Bam.

Sam leapt off the desk and waited for me in the living room, then followed me to the door.

Leesa Bevlov and Steve Zhao stood on the porch, looking hot and grumpy. I motioned for them to come inside.

"I made some iced tea," I said over my shoulder. "Take a seat in the living room and I'll bring some glasses."

Steve thanked me. Bevlov didn't say a word.

A few minutes later, we were gathered in the living room, Bevlov and Steve sitting in the two leather easy chairs and Sam in his favorite spot—the nubby, striped ottoman.

"That's a very large cat you have there." Bevlov studied Sam through narrowed eyes.

"It looks like a cheetah or something," Steve added.

Bevlov scowled. "Please do not tell me it's one of those illegal exotics that can rip your face off."

Sam's ears twitched.

Legal? Yes. Capable of violence? Also yes. "He's a Bengal," I replied.

I poured two glasses of iced tea and handed them to my guests. Bevlov nodded pointedly at Steve, who put down his glass and retrieved a small notebook from a pocket.

"So, let's start at the beginning, shall we?" Bevlov said. "Where were you when you first noticed Cooper loose, and where was he?"

And so it went, Bevlov firing off one question after another until we had reached the moment I discovered Naomi's body in her bedroom.

"And then what did you do?" Bevlov couldn't have sounded more suspicious if she tried.

I took a sip of my tea. "Checked for a pulse, didn't find one, and called you."

"From inside the house?"

I shook my head. "No. From the yard."

Steve scribbled something in his notebook, his expression unreadable.

"I see. You didn't go into any other rooms? Have a little look around?"

"No."

"Mmm." Bevlov raised an eyebrow, clearly not convinced. "What did you make of all that weird artwork?"

She was testing me.

"I didn't notice any weird artwork, but then, I was only inside for a moment."

Bevlov stared at me for a few seconds before continuing.

"Interesting, don't you think? Misty Denner was in horror movies and, from what we understand, was wrapping up a film right next door when she died. Did you know that?"

I nodded. "I heard that, yes. It was all over the news."

"Do you think all that monster stuff on Naomi's walls had anything to do with her job?" Bevlov leaned back in her chair, tapping a nail against the glass of iced tea.

I took a deep breath before replying. "Again, I can't address her artwork." Which was technically true—I wasn't an art expert.

I decided to ask a question of my own. "Can you tell me anything about those bitemarks on the victims?" I asked.

Bevlov bristled. "Who said they were bitemarks? And how did you know the first victim had them?"

The woman was impossible. I shrugged.

"My guy found the body, remember? And I'm no expert, but Naomi's wounds certainly looked like bitemarks to me."

"You're right," Bevlov said. "You *aren't* an expert, and we are *not* prepared to talk about the wounds with…" She seemed to be searching for words.

"Outside agencies?" Steve offered.

Bevlov sniffed loudly. "I would hardly call a bunch of security guards an agency."

Nice. In my house, drinking my tea.

Steve's phone rang. He glanced down at the screen and picked up the call. Bevlov scowled at the interruption.

"Sorry," he said breathlessly. "That was one of the uniforms across the street. He said people are beginning to gather outside the home, asking questions. He wants to know what they should do."

Bevlov opened and closed her mouth. She set her empty glass on an end table. "They can't know about what happened! Not yet. We haven't even released a statement." She glanced at me, her eyes narrowing. "Wait. Did you release something? Without my permission?"

I got up and poured the detective another glass of iced tea. "Permission wasn't required. I'm chief of security for Chavez Ravine. My community needs to know what happened and that the police are responding."

Bevlov seemed momentarily taken aback by my response but quickly regained her composure. "You better not have divulged any critical details."

I just rolled my eyes.

"Well, since you created this mess, you can go over there and handle the crowd yourself. My officers have better things to do than deal with a bunch of nervous looky-loos."

Sam was staring at me intently. He was up to something.

The next moment, he was in the air, leaping onto the couch, extending a paw, and swiping at Bevlov's glass when he flew by. Iced tea cascaded onto her lap.

The detective jumped to her feet with a yelp.

I rushed into the kitchen to fetch a towel.

"I hate cats," Bevlov muttered, dabbing at the giant wet spot on her crotch.

I did not say, "Obviously, the feeling is mutual," but it took every bit of restraint I had.

Bevlov got to her feet, threw the towel on the coffee table, and barked, "Come on, Steven. We're outta here." I noticed the embarrassment in Steve's eyes while they walked out the door.

Halfway down the path, Bevlov stopped and wagged a finger in my direction. "You better get over there quick. I can't spare manpower to deal with the nonsense your little alert caused." She gestured at the gathering crowd of neighbors.

I ignored her. Of course, I would go reassure our residents. I didn't need her to tell me to do that.

But first, I had something important to do.

I hurried into the kitchen and dropped a few salmon nuggets into Sam's bowl. He sauntered over, his tail high in the air. It was probably my imagination, but I could swear he winked at me.

I was so proud of my furry friend that I took a chance and scratched his neck. Sam stiffened, startled, but quickly resumed eating.

When I looked outside the window, Bevlov was standing on the sidewalk across the street, staring back at my house, hands on her hips and a murderous expression on her face.

Chapter 15

By the time the crowd started to break up, I was hot, sweaty, and exhausted. There hadn't been much I could say, but people were more interested in talking than listening anyway.

Mostly, they had wanted to share their outrage that such horrible things could happen in the safe, gated community of Chavez Ravine. I nodded so much my neck started to ache, and my face began to hurt from holding a sympathetic expression for so long.

When I finally made it to my office, Bailey, Liam, and Justin were hanging around outside the door, looking sheepish.

"Ron said we should talk to you," Bailey said without preamble.

I forced a smile to my face. "Oh? What about?"

Liam glanced around nervously. But he wasn't the anxious type. None of them were.

"Come on in." I threw open the door, grateful for the central air that wafted out, cooling my skin. After grabbing four cold water bottles from the mini fridge—one of the perks of my office—I handed them around.

Liam gulped his water, then ran a hand through his damp blond hair. Justin's right knee bounced up and down while Bailey peeled the label from the plastic water bottle.

I took a deep breath, trying to find the patience for what was shaping up to be a difficult conversation. "Look…I've always encouraged open and honest communication on our team, and whatever you have to say, I want to hear it."

The three young guards exchanged glances. Bailey raised her chin.

"Well, that's the thing. We don't think you have been completely honest with us."

That was unexpected.

I leaned back in my chair, my pulse quickening. "What do you mean?"

Bailey shifted in her seat, her eyes never leaving my face. "Well, for one thing, there's Dog Face Bride. We get the sense you know more about her than you're telling us. If she's not an entity, what is she?"

Liam cleared his throat. "One of the reasons I took this job was the Bad Pete viral video, with you taking out those monster birds, and the guys say you've had to get rid of a few other creatures. But you never talk about it, so we got to wondering why."

Before I had a chance to reply, Justin spoke up. "Plus, Ron's said some stuff, you know. About the history of Chavez Ravine and the crazy stuff that used to happen here, like hauntings and whatever and—"

Bailey interrupted. "Ron tells Justin stuff because they're both in the Latino club and we're not."

"There's no club!" Justin snorted loudly. "But yeah, he's more comfortable talking about that old stuff with me. The thing is, none of us know the whole story of what happened here, way back in the day *and* right before we got here. We need to know what we're dealing with."

All three stared at me, waiting for an answer. They had a right to know, of course. And they *were* former Occult Affairs officers who had dealt with all sorts of strangeness. They might be surprised by what I had to say, but they could handle it.

I took a moment to gather my thoughts.

"You're right. There are things that happened in Chavez Ravine that go beyond what you'd consider normal. I'll tell you what I know, but everything I'm about to say stays in this room. Understood?"

"Understood," all three said in unison.

"Okay, yes. This community has a history of supernatural activity going back long before the current entity troubles. Many years ago, when the city was hell-bent on evicting everyone in Chavez Ravine to build a housing project, some of the residents started fighting back. They weren't wealthy or politically connected, but they were smart, and they started getting sympathy from regular Angelenos. The city hadn't expected such a well-organized resistance. One city council member in particular was furious. Turns out, he was a witch from a long line of witches in Ireland. He realized he couldn't shut people up but he *could* try to scare them out, so he conjured up monsters and set them loose."

Justin's dark eyes glittered. "No way. What an asshole."

"A big one, by all accounts." I sipped my water. "Eventually, a young woman by the name of Trini Duran studied the monsters and realized it was possible to take them out, under certain circumstances. She was a good shot, with a gun *and* a slingshot, which was how I got the idea slingshots might work for us too. Trini got a group together to take on the monsters, and they succeeded. They also had some help from Lencha Bantacorte, my great-aunt."

"The bruja," Justin said excitedly. "My grandparents were from Solano Canyon, and even they'd heard about her."

"She's the witch Ron keeps talking about," Bailey muttered.

"Ron says you're one of those too," Liam added. "A bruja."

Justin held up a hand. "Let her finish her story."

"I'll get to that in a minute," I promised. "But yes, Lencha was known as a healer, a curandera. She dispensed cures for the sick and made spells for people who needed help. It's what she learned as a child on a ranch in Mexico and how she made her living as a single woman in La Loma. But she was also a witch. Not an evil hag with a cauldron and a broom, but someone who could use her magical skills against dark forces that threatened the community."

I paused. The next part would be tricky.

"She wasn't the only bruja around. There was a brujo too, and according to the stories, he was jealous of Lencha's abilities. That man has a descendant living today. You should know who he is, but if anyone finds out I told you, I'll be fired, and you'll get a new boss who won't be nearly so charming and supportive. Got it?"

All three nodded eagerly. With their youthful skin and wide eyes, they reminded me of children waiting for the conclusion of a bedtime story.

"He's a respected member of our community, and he sits on the board. His name is Hernan Frias, the retired professor of mystical studies."

"The old guy?" Liam said in disbelief.

"Is he a brujo too?" Justin asked.

I was getting tired of all the explaining. "Yes. But his magic is a little…iffy. He's the one who created Dog Face Bride and the birds in the Bad Pete video, among other things. But since his magic isn't that powerful, we were able to take them out with slingshots."

"This is insane." Bailey gasped. "Why would he do that? He's on the board."

I sighed. "It's complicated, but he has very strong feelings about who should and who should not live in Chavez Ravine. He thinks only people with family from the old days should be allowed to live here. And so—stop me if you've heard this one—he wanted to scare certain residents into leaving."

Justin hooted. "That old dude has some cojones. Are you saying he tried to scare the white people out?"

"Pretty much." I folded my hands on my desk. "We managed to get rid of all his creations, except for Dog Face Bride. She came at me one night, and I got in some good licks, but she got away. I guess she's been hiding ever since."

"From what you've just said, Dog Face seems different from the others," Liam mused. "Any idea why?"

I shook my head. "Not a clue. Hernan doesn't seem to know either. I've asked him to recall it, reverse his magic, but he claims to not know how."

"Do you believe him?" Bailey sat back in her chair and crossed her arms in front of her chest.

I shrugged. "That's a good question. I can't say I trust him, but I think he's in over his head, and that scares him."

"Serves the viejo right," Justin said. "Can't you use your magic to deal with it? Ron said you're a bruja."

"Yeah, I know he did, but he's not completely right. I inherited some skills, but I'm still trying to figure out what I can do and how to do it. It's not like I can snap my fingers and make things go away. I'm learning, but it's not easy. And just so no one gets the wrong impression, you won't see me controlling the elements or cackling as I fly past the moon. Although, both would be cool."

"But you can do potions," Bailey said. "Maybe not with a cauldron, but you made the stuff that went inside the pouches that worked against the Chupacabras and the gnomes."

"Don't forget the ghoul at Muertos Café," Justin added.

Liam was nodding, his eyebrows scrunched. "Yeah. You never explained how you made those. So, if you used magic, that's kind of awesome."

"You'll remember those pouches *sort of* worked on the gnomes." Still, I couldn't help but smile.

Bailey leaned forward, her eyes bright. "Do you think you can whip up something that can help us subdue the Bride? I mean, what if we track her down? Then what?"

The others nodded in agreement.

"I can try, but no promises. Listen, please. All this talk about me and my brujería stays between us. I don't want people getting the wrong idea. This job is hard enough without people thinking I can turn into a crow or something."

Liam opened and closed his mouth. "Can you?"

"No!"

"Oh." Liam's wide shoulders drooped.

Bailey threw her head back. "Wait. We still haven't talked about the murders. Do you think Dog Face Bride could have done it? You found the victim today. Did you get a look at her? Did she have bitemarks too?"

"Yes. That's another thing that needs to stay confidential. Obviously, Dog Face has teeth, and apparently, the M.E. can't say for sure whether the bitemarks are human or animal. So, the Bride is still at the top of our list. And I sincerely hope she's our murderer because, if she's not, there's another possibility that's much worse: we may be dealing with a new type of entity the heatmaps can't pick up."

"The researchers at Occult Affairs were always worried about that. I mean, anything's possible, right?" Liam cracked his knuckles. "I'm in. Let's do this."

Bailey scoffed. "Do what?"

"The boss is going to make one of those pouch things, then we're going to lure Dog Face Bride out of hiding."

Justin turned in his chair to stare at Liam. "And how do we do that?"

Liam shrugged. "With bait. Don't worry. We'll figure it out."

He made it sound so simple.

Chapter 16

My little chat with Liam, Bailey, and Justin had given me plenty to think about while I should have been sleeping. I had hoped Hernan would help us take out Dog Face Bride, but he was useless. Until Liam suggested it, I hadn't considered taking her on myself.

If I were to go about trying to find a magical solution to our Dog Face Bride problem, how would I even start? Lencha's journals had plenty of rituals and spells, but none looked like they would be of any use against a supernatural entity created by a brujo.

I was walking toward the Jeep, carrying my coffee, when it hit me: Hernan Frias didn't know how to recall the Bride, but maybe *I* could if I had the ingredients he had used to make her.

Instead of going to the office, I drove straight to Hernan Frias's home in Palo Verde. The last couple of times I had visited him, I brought food to boost his mood, but I didn't have time.

When I pulled up, a gardener wearing a straw hat and thick gloves was pruning the bougainvillea growing on a trellis at the front of the house. Hernan had chosen a very unusual color scheme for his abode. Black house, bright red door. The vivid pink bougainvillea was striking against the dark paint. I was still surprised the HOA had approved his palette, but I suspected he had called in a favor or two.

After giving a friendly wave to the gardener, I walked up the path. Hernan's caretaker, Marta, answered the door wearing a pinafore apron over a light summer dress.

"You're still here!" I sounded surprised. "I thought Hernan was doing well enough to be on his own."

Marta pursed her lips, leaned forward, and in a low voice said, "He can't handle this house alone."

"Is he around?"

I looked past Marta into the gloomy living room filled with heavy, dark furniture. No sign of Hernan. I got it. It wasn't a space I would want to spend time in either.

"He's in the backyard, taking a nap in the hammock."

"I need to talk with him. Okay if I head back?"

Marta rubbed the side of her face. "Can you go around the side?"

"Of course." I knew the drill—pretend I walked back there on my own, without Marta knowing, sparing her Hernan's fury for letting me in.

Hernan was asleep on the hammock, a straw hat covering his face. It appeared pretty comfortable. If my backyard were larger, I would have been tempted to get one myself.

I cleared my throat.

A brown hand knotted with dark veins lifted the hat. Hernan glared in my direction. "What are *you* doing here?"

"Nice to see you too." I dragged a chair to the hammock. "We need to chat."

Hernan reached into his shirt pocket and pulled out a mobile phone. "See this? Some people use them to call before they show up. If you had, I would have told you I was indisposed."

"Nice word! Funny, I always thought it meant 'in the bathroom.' I guess that's why you're the professor."

He swung his legs over the side and struggled to sit up. "Did you bring me some pan dulce?"

"I didn't have time. This is a bit of an emergency." I stood up, grabbed both his hands in mine, and pulled him upright. He was surprisingly light.

Hernan paled. "What's happened? Is it…her again?"

"We don't know for sure. My team lost her somewhere in Phantom's Pass, but we need to catch her. We've had two murders, and it's possible she's the killer."

"Are you saying both those poor women were *mauled?*" he cried.

I stared at him.

Hernan's eyes widened, then quickly narrowed. His expression turned defensive. "From the very beginning, she was a mistake. She didn't behave like the others, never quite following orders. Defying me."

"Hernan. We need to do something, and by that, I mean we need to get into that shed of yours and get to work."

Hernan's face turned an odd shade of gray. "You have no idea what I went through to bring her to life. I've told you, undoing what has been done is not possible." His voice trembled with indignation.

"I'm not asking you to undo anything, Señor Frias, except work with me. Collaborate."

He wobbled on his feet and gasped. "Collaborate! With you?"

"Yes, with me. You got any better ideas?" I steered him toward the shed.

He muttered under his breath. I could have sworn he called me a pendeja.

"Did you just call me an idiot?" I tightened my grip on his shoulders, kicked open the door of the shed, and gave him a little push inside.

"Quit manhandling me!" he cried.

"Quit your belly aching."

"What do you want from me?"

I pointed at the bags of red clay and masa harina on the workbench. "That. I need you to whip up another batch of the stuff you used to sculpt your creatures, and when you're done, I want you to make another Dog Face."

Hernan shook his head. "Are you loca? I thought you wanted to get rid of her, and now you're asking me to make another one?" His eyes widened. "That doesn't make any sense...unless you want the new creature to kill the old one? Do you? That's never going to work! Who will kill the new one?"

"No, Hernan. That is not what I'm going to do," I said firmly.

He crossed his arms in front of his chest. "Then what is? I'm not doing a darn tootin' thing until you explain yourself."

"Language, please!" I laughed.

He wasn't laughing with me.

"Okay, calm down. We're going to collaborate. You make a little figurine that looks just like a miniature Dog Face Bride, and then I'm going to take it home and see if I can find a way to break the spell that animates the big one. Or something like that."

Hernan scoffed. "You *are* loca! That doesn't even make sense."

It didn't make complete sense to me either, but I was operating on gut instinct. If Little Lencha could help me cast a protection spell over Chavez Ravine, maybe Little Dog Face Bride would help me catch her big, ugly sister.

"Just trust me and do it. What do we have to lose?"

Hernan stared at me in disbelief. "What if your Bantacorte magic blows up and you create an even bigger version?"

He couldn't resist a dig at my family, but he did have a point. Things might go wrong. *Badly* wrong. Just like when I had conjured a mermaid. But I was running out of options.

"We don't have a choice, Hernan. Not if she's our killer."

Hernan let out a heavy sigh and nodded. "Fine. I'll do it. But don't come crying to me for help when things go badly."

I clapped him on the back. "I promise."

He grumbled again in Spanish and began gathering the materials from the shelves. A knot of unease tightened in the pit of my stomach while I watched him work. Hernan's long fingers sculpted clay into the shape of Dog Face Bride, but not easily. Maybe it was arthritis, but he was no Julia Suarez. He lacked her talent and finesse. When he was finally finished, he held up the figurine for me to see. It looked like something a child might have made, but it would have to do.

"Thank you." I plucked it from his hand before he could have second thoughts and headed for the door.

Hernan grabbed my arm. "Where are you going?"

"Home," I said, pulling away. "That's where all my stuff is."

"I thought you said we were going to collaborate! You need to take me with you. I need to see what you get up to."

No, he did not. I didn't need a backseat brujo second-guessing my every move. And I didn't think Little Lencha would have liked it one bit.

I patted his shoulder. "We *did* collaborate. Just now. You contributed your part, and now I'm off to do mine."

I turned on my heel and hurried out the door.

"Brujería isn't a team sport!" Hernan shouted after me.

Chapter 17

On the drive home, Stu called. "Why don't we have dinner someplace, and then you can spend the night?"

I sighed. "That sounds awfully tempting, but I've got a lot of work to do."

"Oh, come on. You can't work twenty-four-seven. You'll burn out. Take a break. With me." He paused. "Or are you worried about leaving that demon cat of yours alone? I can pick up some food, and we can hang out at your place."

The truth was, as much as I wanted to spend more time with Stu, I wasn't comfortable telling him about my magic. He was a down-to-earth, practical guy. I had no idea how he would react to finding out his new girlfriend could conjure mermaids. It was still too early in our relationship for that kind of revelation.

"I'm sorry, but I've had a really long day, and there's still some stuff I need to take care of. Can I take a rain check?" I tried to keep my voice light, regretful.

It was Stu's turn to sigh. "Fair enough. Rain check it is." His voice sounded heavy with disappointment.

"Thanks for understanding." When I ended our call, I couldn't shake off the guilt. Secrets were bad for relationships. I would eventually figure out a way to explain mine, but I couldn't risk it yet.

A few minutes later, Stu called back. "If I ask you a question, will you answer it honestly?"

A knot formed in my stomach. "Of course."

There was a moment of silence on the line, and I could almost hear Stu contemplating his next words.

"I'm getting the impression you're going to have a lot on your plate until these murders are solved. And it's okay. It's fine. I get it. I do. Thing is, my brother and some old buddies invited me to join them on a guys trip to Las Vegas. I told them no because I didn't want to be away from you a whole week. But since you've got your hands full, I was thinking I'd join them, after all. But I won't go if you want me around. Even just for moral support."

The thought of Stu changing his plans for me made my heart do a little happy dance. But the next moment, it crashed. This very nice, sexy man had the impression I was too busy to spend time with him, that I was putting my job before our relationship.

But it wasn't *just* my job. It was fear. Fear of rejection. Fear of losing him when he found out what I was. The thought of walking him through my complicated story and convincing him to stick around while also dealing with two murders was overwhelming. I would do it. Just later.

I pulled into my driveway. A couple walking a dog paused in the street, staring at the crime scene tape on Naomi's porch.

"You're right. Things are going to be crazy for a while. I think you should go and have fun with your brother. I'll be fine, and we can still talk."

A long silence followed. "But you'll miss me, right?" Stu's voice was tinged with uncertainty.

"Of course I will," I said firmly. "I'd much rather spend time with you than track down a killer, believe me."

"Liar," Stu said, then laughed. "Listen, I'm going to call Clare and let her know. I don't want her at the house alone, not with everything going on. She's not getting along with my ex right now, so she probably won't be too happy about it. Hey, stay in touch, okay? Let me know how things are going. I'll be thinking about you the whole week."

"We'll talk," I promised, followed by another stab of guilt. "And have fun. Try not to get into too much trouble."

Stu snorted. "I'll behave, just for you." His voice softened. "Take care of yourself, okay? And don't work too hard."

"Don't *play* too hard," I replied.

I walked up the path. My feet felt like they were encased in lead. When Stu was back—assuming he hadn't been snatched up by a hot divorcee on a singles safari—I would tell him about my magic. But tonight, I needed to focus on catching Dog Face bride.

Inside, I placed Hernan's bad sculpture next to Little Lencha on the workbench in the sunroom. Maybe it was my imagination, but it seemed to me the figurine's clay eyes shifted toward her new companion in a disinterested sort of way.

I had hoped for more of a reaction. A glow, maybe. Or an appearance in the sunroom and an explanation of what I needed to do to catch Dog Face Bride.

But no.

Maybe my mother was right and I had "skipped the line," as she put it, inheriting magic that she'd never had. Even Hernan Frias had said I hadn't earned whatever magic I had acquired because I hadn't put in the time and practice brujería required.

I collapsed into a wicker chair. Obviously, there was something more I needed to do, but what?

Liam had mentioned luring the monster out of hiding. That would be step one. Step two would be taking her out, once and for all.

I had no idea how to do either.

Sam bumped into my legs and meowed loudly, his way of reminding me he was overdue for a treat.

A treat. My cat was a genius!

Dog Face Bride might have been a monster, but she had the face and teeth of a dog. And boy, did dogs like treats.

Okay, maybe it was a longshot, but I didn't have any better ideas.

I rushed into the kitchen, opened the pantry, and took inventory. It was well-stocked. I could make pretty much anything I wanted. But what? What kind of treat would one make for a dog in a wedding dress?

It hit me, standing there, staring into my pantry.

What could be more ridiculous than luring a monster dog with a treat? How about luring a monster dog dressed like a bride with Mexican wedding cookies?

The whole idea was so silly, I started to laugh. Wedding treats for a dog bride. *Hahaha.*

But why not? I had seen weirder things. At worst, there would be a plate of cookies for the crew in the command center the next day.

Out came the pecans, flour, salt, butter, powdered sugar, and vanilla. I mixed everything up and stared at the dough. While I was sure they would be delicious, there was nothing magical in them. They needed a special ingredient to be transformed.

I heard a guttural meow, turned, and saw Sam pawing at the window overlooking the backyard.

"What's wrong with you now, you weirdo?"

He leapt to the floor, ran into the sunroom, and began pounding the French door with his paw.

"Dude, you have *got* to use your litter box more often."

I opened the door and Sam ran out, but he didn't hop over the fence and go to his favorite spot. He ran directly to the habañero plant in my garden.

"You're kidding?"

Sam meowed loudly, seemingly very pleased with himself.

That was all the encouragement I needed. I grabbed a pair of scissors from my workbench, went outside, and snipped off a few of the bright orange chilis.

After dicing and sautéing them in olive oil, I threw them into a blender with some water. When the mixture was thick and smooth, I added the slurry to the cookie bowl. The ball of dough absorbed the chili paste as if it were a living organism hungry to be fed. The dough turned a strange orange color.

I shaped the cookies into little balls and popped them into the oven. When they were done, I rolled them in powdered sugar, placed them on a glass dish, and took them into the sunroom, where I performed a simple ritual, one hand on the cookies, the other clutching the figurine Hernan had made.

I could have sworn Little Lencha's clay head tilted toward me. She had her ways of communicating, though I still wondered if it was all in my head.

When I was done, I covered the dish with plastic wrap. Then I sat down with some of Lencha's notebooks. If all went well, the cookies would lure Dog Face Bride out of hiding, and the chili spell might take some of the fight out of her. But would it be enough to eliminate the creature? I couldn't take any chances. If the treats worked, I would have one shot at that mangy monster, and I needed to get it right.

A few minutes with Lencha's notebooks was all it took.

It was time to go to the command center and organize a hunting party.

The doorbell rang. Whoever it was, I really didn't have time to chat, so I quickly opened the door, ready to shoo away whoever was there.

It was Clare Wells flanked by two classmates. All three wore serious, somewhat sad faces.

"We were hoping you'd be home," Clare said. "I know I should have called first."

"That's all right," I said. Clare—with her mother issues—didn't need any negative vibes coming from her father's girlfriend. "Is everything okay?"

Iris, the tall girl with the straight black hair and Cupid's bow lips, answered. "Clare said we shouldn't bother you. That you'd be busy with everything that's going on. But I said we *had* to see you because we're out of options."

The other girl nodded. "Totally out of options." She was petite, with thick blond hair and round blue eyes.

The girls wore shorts and tank tops. They looked hot and sweaty.

"Did you just come from soccer practice?" I gestured for them to come inside.

All three nodded in unison.

The blond girl looked around, nodding in approval. "I like your house. It's not like I expected. It's not very…witchy. But it's nice."

I glanced over at Clare. Her cheeks flushed with embarrassment. She shifted from foot to foot.

"Sorry. This is Mabel. I kinda told her about you."

Mabel smiled. She had rosy cheeks and perfect white teeth. "Clare told me *all* about you. I mean, I saw for myself what those amulets could do against those nasty things that showed up in the cactus garden, but she explained how your mother is Malena B and that you do something called…ber…" Her voice trailed off, and she looked at Clare.

"Brujería," Clare supplied.

Mabel snapped her fingers. "That's right. Iris and I were looking it up last night."

The last time Clare had shown up with Iris in tow, the dark-haired girl was being bullied by a teammate. One of my amulets had helped. Then Clare asked if I could make her friends in Chavez Ravine entity-protection pouches, like the one I had given her. Those had seemed to work too, although imperfectly.

"Ladies, I'm kind of in the middle of a few things here, so why don't you tell me what's going on, and I'll see if I can help."

Clare's eyes got wide. "Oh, I'm so sorry, Maddy! I knew you'd have a lot going on, with the murders and everything. We shouldn't have come."

She grabbed her friends' elbows and steered them toward the door.

After a rough start, Clare and I were finally getting along, and the last thing I wanted to do was become another adult woman letting her down.

"Wait, Clare. Why don't you tell me what's up, and if there's something I can do quickly, I'll do it."

"Really? Oh, Maddy, thank you! We'll be fast, I promise."

I crossed my arms, trying to appear both patient and supportive.

"So, here's our problem," Clare began in a rush. "We have a big match on Saturday. It's against the Turf Titans, and they're really good. If we lose, it'll be nearly impossible for us to get into the playoffs, so we've been practicing hard this week. Maybe too hard because our goalie took a bad fall and sprained her ankle."

I nodded. And glanced at the clock.

"She's amazing, so if she can't play, we're definitely going to lose. That's why we were wondering if there was a kind of potion or spell or something that you could make to help fix her ankle."

All three girls gazed at me with hopeful expressions. Fortunately, I had an idea.

"Wait here. I'll be back in a couple of minutes."

Finally, something I was confident I could actually do. The girls needed a cure, not a spell. I went straight to Lencha's curandera notebooks and quickly found the recipe for an ankle poultice. At my workbench, I ground the pungent herbs and seeds on a metate, then added them to a few ounces of mentholated ointment. I closed my eyes, said some words of healing and good luck, then scraped the mixture into a small glass jar and placed it in a paper sack.

"Smear the paste on your goalie's ankle right where it hurts, then wrap it with a fresh bandage." I handed Clare the bag. "Have her keep that on for twenty-four hours, and when she takes it off, she should feel better. She might not smell so great, but the pain should be gone."

Mabel's brow furrowed. "That's it?"

I laughed while I moved them toward the door. "You were expecting an eye of newt and some dragon's blood? Sorry to disappoint you! This is the kind of cure my ancestors have been making for generations, so it's time-tested."

I was waving at them while they walked under the hot sun to Clare's SUV when a thought occurred to me. "You're not planning on staying at your dad's place tonight, are you?" I called after them.

The three stopped in their tracks and exchanged nervous glances.

Busted.

Clare blinked rapidly. "Uh, no."

"Clare Wells, you know what's going on around here. Under no circumstances are any of you to stay alone, anywhere, in Chavez Ravine. If I find out otherwise—and I have my methods—I *will* be calling your father." The words rolled off my tongue.

I narrowed my eyes at her, making sure she knew I meant business.

Clare nodded. "We won't. I promise." The girls quickly piled into the car and drove off.

Another thing to worry about. Questionable promises from children who were not my own.

Chapter 18

I had lost valuable time. So I dialed Ron and told him to pick up Bailey and meet me at Phantom's Pass, the most likely place for Dog Face Bride to hang out during the day.

Then I called Liam and requested that he stop by a store to grab a few things, plus Justin, and head for the pass.

With the plate of cookies and Hernan's little figure riding shotgun, I drove past Stu's house, just to make sure Clare and her friends hadn't decided to pull a fast one and stay the night. Clare's SUV was nowhere to be seen. That was good. If it had been in the driveway, I don't know what I would have done. Probably risked damaging my relationship with her because I was trying to protect her.

Which, I realized, was a choice parents must have to make all the time.

I had one stop left on my way up the hill. When I pulled into Ben Tomas's nursery and explained what I was looking for, Ben ran to his shed and returned seconds later. He put two boxes into the back of the Jeep.

The sun was low in the sky by the time I parked near the entrance. The hills were full of shadows.

Phantom's Pass was a dip in the ridge at the top of Bishop. On one side was Chavez Ravine, and on the other was the wooded expanse of Elysian Park. Hiking trails crisscrossed all through the area, but the road ended just below the pass. We would have a short hike to get to the top.

When the others arrived, we split up the cargo. With help from Justin, Liam carried the supplies he had bought. Ron and Bailey each snatched a box from the back of the Jeep, and I held the plate of cookies and the crude clay Dog Bride figurine Hernan had created.

Despite the shade from the trees, it was still hot. By the time we got to our destination—a clearing at the top of the hill—my cotton shirt was damp with sweat and sticking to my back.

Ron, wearing one of his ridiculous camo outfits, jogged over and took the plate from my hands. "Nice! You brought snacks. I love these cookies. My grandma makes them."

I rolled my eyes. "They're lures to bring our friend out of hiding, Ron."

The others came over and looked inside the container too.

"You sure made a lot of them," Justin said. "Maybe if there's any left over, we can have some?"

Bailey lightly punched his arm. "Can you guys please think about catching this thing instead of feeding your faces?"

"Hey, we can multitask." Justin opened one of the boxes and lifted out a garden sprayer Ben had given me. He held it up for inspection. "We gonna take her out with fertilizer?"

Sometimes, it was just better not to engage.

Liam brought out a paper grocery bag with the vinegar, hydrogen peroxide, and water bottles I had requested. "How much of this stuff do we add?"

I gave him the proportions I had researched on the internet, then reached into the sprayer boxes and pulled out face masks and gloves.

"Put these on. This stuff is dangerous, so don't get it on your skin, don't breathe the vapors, and don't spray your teammates."

Liam, looking a little freaked out, poured the chemicals into the first cannister.

"It stinks." Liam pulled his head back. "And it's bubbling. I guess that's good."

Ron nodded while Liam added liquid to the second container. "Now what?"

I pulled out Hernan's clay figurine and set it on the ground in the middle of the clearing. Next to it, I added the plate of Mexican wedding cookies.

"Those look kinda orange," Ron said. "What did you do to them?"

"What do you think?" Bailey wriggled her fingers in the air. "Her witchy stuff."

Ron groaned. "For the hundredth time, it's brujería."

"That's easy for you to say." Bailey sniffed. "I can't roll my r's."

I sat back on my heels and studied our little trap. Outside, in the open air, the aroma of the cookies couldn't compete with the rich, loamy smells of the forest. How was Dog Face Bride to know the yummy goodness awaited?

Sam popped into my mind. He could hear the rustling of the treat bag three rooms away.

Perhaps I was taking this thing too far. Treats to lure a dog monster. Wedding cookies because she wore a bridal gown. And now the rustling of a treat bag to get her attention. It was all too…I don't know…*simple*. Obvious. It couldn't possibly work. And if it failed, I would feel like a fool.

Which is exactly what it was like working for Occult Affairs, carrying a purple Smoke Bomb and pulling a crate to deal with who knew what kind of entity. It was almost comical—the opposite of what most people think of as a police bust. No battering ram, no body armor, no high-powered weapons with someone yelling, "Go! Go! Go!" while officers streamed into a building.

Just me, my pouch, and my soothing voice. But as silly as it might have looked, it worked.

Which is probably why a phrase from my training kept running through my head. Words that had been designed to make me forget how I looked and focus instead on what I was doing.

In for a dime, in for a dollar.

Once you've decided what you're going to do, execute.

It was time for me to fully commit. I gathered some pebbles from the ground, dropped them into the empty shopping bag, stood up, and shook it. Even I could have mistaken it for a bag of kibble.

Bailey grinned and pumped her sprayer to build up pressure. "I get what you're doing."

"That's why she's the boss," Ron said.

"Suck up," Justin muttered.

Liam spun around, frowning. "I think I hear something," he whispered.

"That was fast." Ron sounded panicked.

Bailey and Liam each grabbed a sprayer, and we scattered in all directions.

I crouched behind an enormous rock and scanned the area for my team. They were well hidden.

A growl rumbled, followed by the snapping of dry twigs. Leaves rustled. I had my magic, and we had two sprayers filled with caustic liquid, slingshots, and batons, just in case. We were ready.

"Wait for my signal, then hit the thing with the sprayers as quickly as you can," I whispered loudly.

A figure stepped out from behind a large oak tree. Dog Face Bride had arrived. Her dress was dirtier and more tattered than I remembered. She was taller, and the parts of her that were human—her arms and legs—seemed to have aged.

Snout in the air, she sniffed a few times, then made straight for the plate of cookies.

When she reached it, she stared down at the clay figurine, threw her head back, and howled. The sound sent shivers down my spine. It was a primal, guttural expression of rage and sadness. It brought tears to my eyes, and I cursed Hernan under my breath.

He had done this. The man had created a monster, and it had followed his orders. A monster that might have killed two women in Chavez Ravine. A creature that was lost and alone.

Dog Face gave the figurine a mighty kick, sending it flying. It smacked into the trunk of a tree and exploded into bits.

Apparently, we had similar opinions about Hernan's artistic skills.

The creature dropped to all fours, pushed her snout into the bowl, and began to eat. After a moment, her enormous head came up, eyes glazed. One habañero too many, perhaps?

She snapped her jaws, lowered her head, and continued eating. Ravenously. When she was done, she staggered to her feet, swaying back and forth like a drunken sailor. Foam dripped from her mouth, and she stumbled toward the pine trees. The chilis and the spell were doing their work. Time for the real test.

I closed my eyes and tried to clear my mind, just like I had at the pond, picturing Dog Face Bride coming toward me, growling and drooling…My chest swelling with power, building up a great charge I could unleash on the monster.

Then I opened my eyes. I had been half right: the Bride *was* coming my way.

I closed my eyes again and mustered all my mental energy, focusing on the Bride getting hit with my unstoppable power, falling back, writhing and withering from my mighty blast. I opened one eye.

The bride was getting closer.

Once again, I closed my eyes. I squeezed them so hard the muscles in my forehead ached.

Please, Lencha, send me the magic I need!

My breathing became shallow, and my heart began to race. My shoulder muscles tightened, and I raised my arms into the air, willing the energy in my chest to flow through my hands and to its target. I let out a yell and shook my arms as hard as I could.

When I opened my eyes, Dog Face Bride was so close I could smell her foul breath. There had been no burst of energy, nothing flowing from my fingertips to stop the beast in her tracks. Just a crazy forty-year-old woman yelling and flinging her arms around.

Screw it.

"Now!" I shouted.

Liam sprang from behind a tree and reached her first, aiming the sprayer directly at her head and blasting. The mixture hit her square in the face. She threw up her paws and let out an unearthly cry.

Bailey joined in the attack. The creature snarled and charged at me, jaws snapping, but Bailey cut her off, her sprayer releasing a stream of the caustic liquid. Ron came running out, brandishing his baton, but his foot hit a rock, and he went sprawling, landing at Dog Face's clawed feet. Not that she seemed to notice; she was pawing at her eyes, writhing in agony.

Ron scrambled to his feet and drew back his baton.

But the creature had been reduced from a menacing figure to something pitiful. In unspoken agreement, we all stepped back.

The gray visage of Dog Face Bride turned as red as one of Julia's clay sculptures, and she began to melt before our eyes.

Ron was the first to break our silence. "That's that. then."

It was. But instead of a sense of accomplishment, all I felt was disappointment.

My magic had let me down.

Chapter 19

I didn't have tire tracks on my back when I woke up the next morning, but by about eight thirty, I sure did.

Because, at a televised press conference, Detective Leesa Bevlov threw me under the bus.

She had just finished her slow, plodding recitation of the facts of Naomi Taylor's death—another fatal broken neck ruled a homicide—and opened the conference up for questions.

"Can you tell me what the LAPD has done to ensure the safety of the residents in Chavez Ravine?" a reporter asked.

Bevlov pursed her lips. "Chavez Ravine is a private community. We have no jurisdiction, except when investigating crimes. They have their own team up there responsible for day-to-day security."

"Can you tell us what measures they took to keep residents safe after the Misty Denner murder?"

"I cannot. Their security force is a private organization, and they do not share their protocols with us. We are simply the investigating agency."

Another reporter spoke up. "Isn't their head of security a former officer with Occult Affairs?"

Bevlov gave a curt nod. "Yes, that's right. Her name is Madeline Madrigal. If you have any more questions about their security—or lack thereof—I suggest you contact her directly."

I shouted at the TV screen and spilled my coffee all over my lavender trench coat. Even Sam jumped, and my cat did not startle easily. Anger bubbled inside me like a raging inferno. If I hadn't been holding my favorite mug, I would have thrown it at the screen. The audacity of Bevlov to suggest that, somehow, our guards could have prevented the murders was *beyond* comprehension.

Sam sat on a windowsill, licking a paw and eyeing me warily.

"I am not being dramatic," I said. "My day just went straight to shit."

Two seconds later, my phone rang, and it didn't stop for the next hour. Calls from reporters…From Julia and Leo, who had seen the news conference and wanted to share their outrage and support…From a hysterical Eileen Simpson who said she would never be able to sell another house in what she called the murder capital of California.

I put off giving the reporters a statement until I could chat with Cora Bernal. No use going off half-cocked and getting myself into trouble with the woman who signed my paychecks.

But first, I requested a quick meeting with my team. Thanks to Bevlov, residents were sure to be nervous and would want to know what we were doing to keep them safe. I had an idea and wanted input from everyone else.

There was no time for a pit stop at Muertos Café for some pan dulce. As soon as my staff saw me walking in without a pink box in my hands, their expressions fell.

Justin didn't wait for the meeting to start. "My wife is freaking out. She wants to take the baby and stay with her parents for a while."

Ron turned to Bailey, who was picking at a skull decal on a nail. "Aren't you scared? You live alone. You're a woman."

Bailey snapped her head up. "Your powers of observation never fail to amaze me. No, I'm not afraid. I installed a nice little DIY trip wire system, and if anyone gets past it, I'm taking them out with my baton."

Justin scoffed. "Oh, come on. A trip wire? Really?"

"Yes, really." Bailey grinned. "I can handle myself just fine. In fact, I was going to suggest we offer to set them up for the women living alone in Chavez Ravine, who want one."

I had been hoping for suggestions to make residents feel safer, but trip wires didn't seem like the way to go. If someone got hurt, we would be liable. When I explained that, Bailey's shoulders slumped.

"I hadn't thought of that. Bummer."

Ron groaned. "Oh, come on. It's a great idea. Those things won't kill anybody, and they're easy to install. And it would give people a sense of security. We could even offer demos in the community center."

With my luck, Eileen Simpson would get tangled up in hers and break a hip.

"It's out of the question. Too risky. But we *can* offer security walk-throughs. Help them identify weak spots in their homes and reinforce those areas—"

Liam leaned forward in his chair, frowning. "Shouldn't we be opening up that offer to *all* homeowners and not just women living alone? There are plenty of nervous families too."

"Good point." I nodded. "Let's do that. Bailey, can you write up a plan for home evaluations?"

Bailey nodded and started making notes on her phone.

I continued. "Hopefully, we neutralized the killer when we did away with Dog Face Bride, but we need to remain vigilant, just in case." I turned to Ron and Brandon. "You two are still staying on top of the camera feeds, right? If that creepy guy I saw in the gully the night of the first murder is still out there, we need to find him."

Brandon nodded. "Yes, we watch in real time and review the overnight footage every morning, in case the late shift misses something."

"You thought he could have had monster makeup on, right? Maybe he was from that movie Misty Denner was in," Liam added. "Plus, you said Naomi Taylor worked at the studios. Maybe someone on the movie crew is our guy, assuming the Bride wasn't."

I had wondered the same thing but had prioritized the Dog Face Bride. Besides, as Bevlov had made clear, it was not my case. If she found out I was poking around at the studio, who knew how she would retaliate? Things were bad enough as they were. Still, maybe it was time for a conversation with actress Becca Tey, who might know a thing or two.

"You're a horror buff," I said to Liam. "I have no objection if you'd like to do a little research to find out who else is working on that movie. Didn't I hear something about a curse? Apparently, all sorts of odd things have happened."

Liam nodded. "I can do that. I can *totally* do that."

After the team dispersed, I headed straight to Cora's house. She led me across the living room, with its pale walls and beige carpet, and into the colorful kitchen.

The tantalizing aroma of shrimp filled the air. Cora flipped them in the pan. The spice from chili mingled with the sweetness of caramelizing onions and bell pepper.

Bevlov's press conference had ruined my appetite, but Cora's cooking revived it. While she scooped the fajitas onto a large serving dish, my stomach rumbled. Cora quickly set out bowls of guacamole, shredded cheese, and a salad. The flour tortillas were thick and warm.

"Looks amazing! I hope you didn't go through all this trouble just for me."

Cora settled in across from me with a frown. "I did make it for you. And after that nonsense on the TV this morning, I thought you could use a little pick-me-up."

I tore off a section of tortilla and used it to scoop up the fajitas. Cora was old-school Mexican, just like my family, and she would think it odd if I carefully filled and folded my tortilla.

"I haven't had fajitas in a long time. They're amazing. Thank you."

We enjoyed our food in silence for a few moments. When I picked up my second tortilla, I told Cora how we had dispensed with Dog Face Bride.

She pressed a palm to her heart with a gasp. "That's very, very good news! That means your magic is coming along nicely, just like we'd hoped. But I wonder if she was the killer? Frankly, I suspect she wasn't. Now, wouldn't it be something if you could use your powers to find out who murdered those poor women and put a stop to him before he has a chance to do it again?"

Cora's confidence in my skills was flattering, but there was a gap wider than Phantom's Pass between her expectations and my magical capabilities.

"Yes, it would be nice," I began dryly, "but finding a human bad guy requires a different set of skills. As far as I know, not even my great-aunt Lencha could do that."

"You could ask your mother," Cora said. "She's a famous psychic, after all."

I hardly thought tarot card readings qualified. And her psychic connection to entities wouldn't help either. But I didn't want Cora to assume my mommy issues were getting in the way.

"I *could* ask her."

Cora set her fork down and sighed. "This is all our fault. The board's, I mean. We should have sent an alert after the first murder, like you wanted. It sent the wrong message, set a bad tone. I'm afraid you're paying for it now. We had an emergency session after the press conference this morning. We just want you to know we understand the police are in charge and there is very little you and your team can do with a madman on the loose."

I picked up our empty plates, set them in the sink, then turned to face Cora. "The whole board felt that way? Even Eileen Simpson?"

"Charlie and Hernan were able to talk some sense into her."

"Hernan?" My voice rose. "Hernan came to my defense? I have to say, I'm very surprised."

Cora nodded. "I was too. But you know how temperamental he is. Who knows how he'll feel about things a few hours from now?"

She was right. Still, her reassurance lifted a weight from my shoulders.

Cora got up and opened the refrigerator. "Iced coffee?"

"Yes, please!"

Of course, Cora being Cora, it wasn't just regular iced coffee. It came with a drizzle of Mexican chocolate, a sprinkling of chili powder and cinnamon, and a piloncillo sweetener. It was tough not to chug it in a few greedy gulps.

Once again, my thoughts returned to the press conference. "The thing I can't figure out is why Detective Bevlov seems to have it out for me."

"That woman was out of line. What she said was totally uncalled for." The words came out stiffly. Cora stared into her drink.

She might have been the genius behind a tamale restaurant empire, but she was as transparent as a pane of glass. And by the haunted look that had come to her eyes and the way she couldn't stop swallowing, Cora seemed guilty as hell.

I pushed my empty glass away. "Is there something you're not telling me?"

"Well…" Cora's voice trailed off.

A sigh escaped my lips. Cora and her secrets.

"I can't imagine what you might have to say about Bevlov, but whatever it is, I'd really like to hear it."

Cora opened and closed her mouth. She bit her lip, then rubbed her nose. I really wanted to play poker with her one day.

"Cora, please. There's a lot at stake here—and not *just* my professional reputation. With two murders, we should be working together to find the killer, but that's not happening. If you know anything that could help solve that problem, you need to tell me."

The board president gave a half-hearted shrug. "I honestly don't think that will ever happen. Not unless a new detective is assigned to the case."

Talk about cryptic. "And why would that be?"

"Because Detective Bevlov is the one who suggested we create a new head of security position for Chavez Ravine. I'd met her a few times at our downtown restaurant, and we got to talking. The more she learned about our story, the more persuasive she became. Obviously, we decided to create the position, and I immediately thought of you for the job. Because of your…special qualifications. But Detective Bevlov had someone else in mind." Cora grimaced.

My heart sank. "Oh no. Don't tell me."

"That's right. She made it clear *she* wanted the job, and she was quite aggressive about it. Emails. Calls. And when that didn't work, she demanded to pitch her qualifications in front of a full board meeting. I refused, of course. By then, I'd realized she…Let's just say I realized she wouldn't be a good fit for our organization.

"But, unfortunately, she didn't take the rejection well. When she learned we were going with another candidate, she called and gave me an earful. She accused me of stealing her idea and said I would regret not hiring her. Which only confirmed I made the right decision, of course.

"Later, I learned why she wanted the job so badly. She and her husband live in an area of Echo Park that's overrun with entities. She wanted to move to Chavez Ravine, if you can imagine that. In fact, it was her idea to offer subsidized housing to our security team."

Whoa. No wonder Leesa Bevlov couldn't stand the sight of me. "Did you hear from her again after she learned I got the job?"

Cora frowned. "Repeatedly. She said over and over that I'd made a big mistake, that you were underqualified for the position. She even ranted about giving legacy candidates priority."

"She knew I was legacy?"

"*I* certainly never said anything," Cora replied. "But somehow, she found out. I guess that's what detectives do. I wouldn't be surprised if it came from a member of our own board."

I sat back in my chair, trying to process this new information. Detective Bevlov had a personal grudge against me because she believed I had stolen a job out from under her.

She was going to be a giant pain in my ass at every opportunity. And there was nothing I could do about it.

Chapter 20

Bevlov called the next morning. I was in the shower, but she left a message saying Steve was headed over to pick up the surveillance camera footage. And if I had an issue with that, I could call the chief. She made it sound like I had been refusing to share the video, even though this was the first time she had requested it.

I got to my office in Palo Verde Plaza and made an espresso using the fancy machine on the credenza. Was the machine Bevlov's suggestion too? Just thinking that was a possibility made the coffee all the more delicious.

My phone chimed with a text from Stu.

Miss you and have a few minutes. Can you talk?

I dialed his number, like an anxious teenager eager to hear his voice.

"How's Vegas?" I asked.

"Insane," Stu said. "All that noise and smoke in the casinos…The pool's nice, but it's like an oven outside. The guys love it, though, and it's great hanging out with them."

I set the phone on speaker and added a splash of cream to my coffee. "Hitting any clubs?"

Stu scoffed. "Our club days are behind us. Hey, I was catching up on the news and saw the detective calling you out. That was total, one hundred percent bullshit."

"Yeah. She's a piece of work. But at least I found out why she has an issue with me." I went on to explain what I had learned from Cora.

Stu chuckled. "Oh man. Wow. Detective Bevlov isn't doing herself any favors. Cora Bernal knows a lot of people in this town, including city officials, and this could come back to haunt Bevlov. Not to mention, she's shortchanging her investigation by treating you like the enemy."

"Cora knows a lot of people?"

"Of course she does. Everybody who's anybody eats at her restaurant downtown. And Cora knows how to work the dining room, doing the meet and greet. She's very charming."

There was no doubt about that. "Have you heard from Clare?"

"Constantly." Stu sighed. "She's mad I left her with her mother and wants me to come home. As in, right away." He paused. "Have you heard from her?"

"Yes. She was having a friend problem, and she came to see me. Not alone. Iris and Mabel were with her."

"Sounds like they ganged up on you."

A voice in the background shouted Stu's name.

"Hey. I'm sorry, but I better go. We've got a tee time at some fancy golf club. Miss you. Talk soon, okay?" He hung up.

I sipped my coffee, thinking about the craziness of the past few days. Two murders. Bevlov losing her mind. Stu in Vegas because I was too busy to spend time with him. Clare and her friends seeking magical help. None of those things were connected, but they all added to my agitation.

One thing was clear: I needed to focus on keeping the community safe, and since Bevlov didn't seem any closer to finding a suspect, I needed to step up my game.

While I finished my drink, there was a knock, and my door opened a crack. It was Steve Zhao, seemingly ruffled. "Sorry for the rush, but can I get that footage from you?"

I waved him inside. "Good morning to you too."

He stepped past me, glanced around, and gave a low whistle. "This is your office? Wow. You should see the cubicle where I usually work, although the bullpen is worse."

"I've seen both, and I agree with you." I pointed at a seat opposite me. "The bullpen sucks."

Steve lowered himself into a chair. "Is that why you transferred to Occult Affairs?"

"That's a long story. You look like you could use a coffee. Want one?"

"That would be great." Steve sat back. "It's been a long morning already."

Clearly, he wanted to talk. I started making an Americano.

"A long morning in Occult Affairs Research? That always seemed like a low-stress place to me."

"Yeah, it's not too bad, but I'm talking about Bevlov. I guess one of her guys asked her for the surveillance video, and she didn't have it. Because she never asked for it. But that's not what she said. She said I'd screwed up and she'd straighten me out. I wasn't there, but a buddy told me what she said."

I placed a cup under the espresso spigot. "That sucks. I'm sorry it happened."

"Thanks." Steve raked a hand through his hair. "I shouldn't be telling you all this. My friends say I should just go in and tell the chief, but honestly, I don't think he wants to hear it. Any time anyone goes in to complain about a problem, he says—"

I finished his thought. "What do you think this is, fifth grade?"

Steve visibly relaxed, even cracked a smile. "You've heard that before?"

"Only a hundred times." I set the steaming cup of coffee on a little round table next to him. "I think you're right. Complaining will just get another bullseye on your back. Hopefully, your team will find out who killed those women, and you'll be back on the nerd squad."

Steve flinched. "Is that the way everyone talks about us?"

"No. Just every Occult Affairs officer. Don't take it personally. Insults are how people show affection in that place."

Steve took a sip of his coffee and sighed. "Honestly, I can't wait to get back there. I don't know what it is with Bevlov, but she's not nice. And she doesn't play fair."

I fished out a flash drive from a drawer and flicked it across the desk. "I've had this ready for a couple of days. Everything you want is on there, but if you have any questions, give me a call."

"Wow, thanks. That was quick."

"Since you're here, I have a question. Purely theoretical, of course."

Steve raised his eyebrows. "This should be good."

"Far-fetched is more like it. Did you happen to see that poster of the werewolf in Naomi Taylor's bedroom?"

"Hard not to." Steve wrinkled his nose. "She was into some weird stuff."

I couldn't help but laugh. "Things don't get much darker than what you've dealt with, but okay. Just hear me out. I am not saying we're dealing with a werewolf, but those bitemarks and that poster got me thinking. Is there any chance, in your expert opinion, that we could be dealing with the new type of entity you and your buddies over in research have predicted? Entity 2.0?"

Steve removed his glasses and wiped them on the front of his shirt. "I had the same thought. I tried telling Bevlov that, but she didn't want to hear it. She said entities might hurt people, but they didn't enter houses and weren't smart enough to stake out their victims and find a hidden entry point."

"But a new kind of entity *might* be smarter."

Steve stuck his glasses back on. "That's exactly what I said, but she's convinced we're dealing with a human monster."

"A human who can scale walls and who smells like something died?"

Steve got up and began pacing in front of my desk. "She's not big on listening. She's made up her mind." He glanced over at me with a grimace. "Between you and me, I'm worried. I saw a lab report, and they found a few hairs under Taylor's nails. The techs have never seen anything like it. They found unusual patterns and cells, which suggested it's not fully human, but not any kind of animal we know about either."

He took another swig of his coffee.

"Are we talking about a new entity?"

"Maybe." Steve shrugged. "We've been all over Naomi's house, looking for more hairs. Nothing inside. We found a few stuck to the side of the house, below the bedroom window, which suggests her attacker scaled the wall."

Steve's eyes met mine.

"I think it's possible we're looking at a werewolf entity."

I felt dizzy. Any new entity might bring unknowns—would it be immune to my protection spell or to Smoke Bombs?—but a werewolf that could scale walls and enter buildings was terrifying.

"At least, we can't rule it out at this point," Steve said quickly. "I sneaked a copy of that lab report to one of my buddies in OA research, and they're looking into it. If Bevlov finds out, she'll kill me. The crime scene techs have already been over that bit of woods behind the townhouses and the areas near Misty Denner's place, but I'm going to take a look myself. If it *is* a new type of entity, it could have a different emergence pattern."

I thought for a moment. "That's a lot of ground to cover on your own."

"Yeah, but I'm not exactly getting any support from my boss." He stopped pacing and cast a hopeful glance in my direction. "If I were to call in a few favors from my nerd buddies, what would you say? Would you let us search the woods behind the victims' homes?"

I sighed. As much as I disliked the idea of more OA researchers on the loose in Chavez Ravine, I owed it to the community to keep everyone safe. "Yes, but make it quick and keep a low profile."

Steve let out a huge breath. "I promise. Thank you. Thank you *so* much."

Before I could say another word, he grabbed the flash drive from the desk and dashed out of my office.

If the board found out I had let more OA nerds in, Cora might not be able to save me a second time.

Chapter 21

All eyes followed Becca Tey when she crossed the dining room at Olga's Cantina. She was dressed in a loose cream-colored jumpsuit, her dark hair hanging down her back. And while her skin was a little too stretched, her brows a little too high, and her lips unnaturally puffy, Becca had something few people did: an irresistible magnetism.

Others bent their heads together and whispered.

"That's Becca Tey!"

"She was in that vampire soap opera, right?"

Becca slipped into the seat across from me and stared at the glass of white wine in front of her. "Is this for me?"

I nodded. "It's pinot grigio. I hope that's okay."

"More than okay. I'll drink anything after the day I've had."

"That bad?"

"The *worst*. I went to a meeting about a reboot of a show I used to be on. I was thinking they'd pick up where we left off and I would be playing the same character. But that's not the idea at all. The producers want to update the story, so they thought it would be fun if I played the mom. I'm like, okay, but then some twenty-year-old asshole said I was too old and I would make a better grandmother."

"He said that in front of you?" I actually gasped.

Becca picked up her glass. "Without batting an eye."

"One of these days, he'll say that to the wrong person." I dragged a tortilla chip through a bowl of salsa roja. "This wouldn't happen to be the vampire show, would it?"

"You've seen it?" Becca appeared pleased.

I cleared my throat. "Not really, but I've heard about it."

"It's where I first met Misty. She was in the first season. She was already pretty well-known as a scream queen, and the producers thought casting her might get some buzz. It worked, but Misty didn't like the grind of working on a TV series, so she didn't renew, and they had to kill off her character. We stayed friends, though."

Becca picked up the menu and flipped through the pages, scrunching her forehead. Olga's Cantina offered the usual suspects on the typical Mexican menu, plus choices that bewildered non-Latinos.

"I'm sick of salads. What can I have that doesn't have a lot of carbs?"

I didn't even have to look at the menu to answer. "Get the machaca. It's made from flank steak, so it's relatively low-cal. And they really know how to make it here. All you need to do is decide whether you want it with or without egg."

Becca wrinkled her nose. "Like, an over-easy egg on top?"

"Nope. It's scrambled in. I like it that way, but it's just as good without."

After we had placed our orders for machaca, one with and one without egg, I said, "Thank you for agreeing to meet with me. This is my treat, by the way. If I can just ask that you keep our conversation confidential, I would appreciate that."

Becca raised her arched eyebrows. "Are you talking about that detective?"

"Yes."

"I can't stand the woman. No problem."

"Thank you." I sipped my wine. "I'm wondering how much you've heard about the movie *Phantom's Pass*. From Misty or anyone else."

"Well, Misty seemed to be enjoying herself. She had worked with the directors before, and she really liked their vision, the way they approached the horror genre. As she got older, she began to appreciate the more psychological aspects of those stories." Becca gave a grim laugh. "I mean, even scream queens get older, right? But because she was so darn petite, she could get away with playing young longer than most women. She was also blessed with beautiful skin, and she took very good care of it. She rarely drank and never stepped outside without SPF-a-million on her face."

"I heard people say the movie was cursed," I pressed. "That worrisome things were happening on the set."

Becca shrugged. "Yeah. I heard that too. But to be honest, I assumed it was something the PR people had put out there. You know, create a mystery to sell tickets."

"What did Misty say?"

"She didn't worry about those things. She was more concerned that the directors' last movie didn't do so well, and she thought the producers were staging things to make it *look* like there was a curse the actors could talk about in interviews. That kind of stuff can go viral. But then Misty broke her ankle by tripping over a piece of equipment left lying around, and there was only one person to blame for that: a careless grip."

I thought for a moment. "Did Misty ever talk about Naomi?"

Becca shook her head. "Not that I remember."

"You wouldn't happen to know anyone who works on the movie, do you? Someone who would be willing to talk with me?"

Becca drained her wine and held a manicured hand up to summon a server. "Actually, I do. The editor. She was an assistant editor on a series I used to work on, and we've kept in touch. Want me to reach out to her?"

"I would really appreciate that."

Becca's dark eyes narrowed. "Good. Because someone needs to figure out who killed these women before he strikes again, and I don't have much faith in that Bevlov woman."

Chapter 22

My first visit to an actual movie studio was a disappointment. Western Movie Studios, located over the hill from the Bishop neighborhood in Chavez Ravine, was not the least bit glamorous. Nothing but a bunch of old warehouses and the occasional person walking hurriedly between them.

I found the editor of the movie in a 1940s-era two-story wooden building in bad need of a paint job. I parked my Jeep in a small lot and walked across the pavement to a door marked "Sinister Films."

Nothing subtle about that.

Inside, a long hallway with faded red linoleum led to the back of the building. The front door slammed shut while I walked down the hall. Most of the doors on either side were closed.

A woman's voice called out, "If your name is Maddy, I'm back here."

"Back here" turned out to be a windowless room lit by a single floor lamp and the glow from a bunch of screens, the largest mounted on the wall. There was a frozen image of a small group of people sitting around a campfire in the woods, holding beer bottles, looking happy and relaxed.

"Are you Didi Booth?"

A woman spun around in her black leather chair. She was in her mid-fifties, with bangs and silver-streaked brown hair chopped off at her chin. "That's me. I'm the only one here at the moment. The rest are shooting some pickup scenes in Phantom's

Pass, which, considering what I saw this morning, is probably a bad idea."

Didi gave a quick, high-pitched laugh and leaned back in her chair.

"Don't mind me. I'm a little on edge with everything that's happened."

I sidled into the room. It was a cluttered mess. A pile of paper was stacked next to the keyboard. Yellow sticky notes covered every surface. A tower of disc drives threatened to topple over.

My first impression had been wrong. There *was* a window, but it was covered with black fabric held in place by pushpins. A lumpy-looking sofa squatted against the wall.

Didi wore gold cargo pants, purple sneakers, and a purple T-shirt. She gestured to a leather easy chair patched with gray duct tape.

"Thank you for agreeing to see me. I appreciate it." I sat on the edge of the chair, trying not to get tape stuck to my trench coat.

"Anything for Becca," she said. "We go way back. If she says you're good people, I believe it."

I stared at the frozen video on the wall for a moment. "Misty wasn't in that scene?"

"No. That's the scene where she goes off to the bathroom by herself and sees the monster for the first time. Except no one believes her because they think she's taken too many of her meds."

"What did you see this morning that makes you think it was a bad idea for the crew to go back to Phantom's Pass?"

Didi sighed. "I probably shouldn't have said anything, but now that I've opened my big mouth, I'll show you. What the hell. Almost the entire crew saw it, so I figure it's just a matter of time before it starts making the rounds. Which does make me a little suspicious someone staged this. Here. Let me show you."

The conversation wasn't going at all like I had expected. But I was happy to watch whatever it was that bothered her.

"Sure. I'm curious now," I murmured.

Didi hit some buttons, then pointed at the large screen on the wall. "Watch this. Keep your eye on the grove of trees just beyond where the cast is standing. Ready?"

My pulse quickened. Didi was good at her job; she knew how to build suspense.

"Ready."

Didi hit play, and the video began running. Four people stood in the clearing, looking around nervously. Closest to the grove in the background was Misty Denner wearing hiking gear, her petite frame dwarfed by her much taller companions. The group began to argue about which direction to take, with Misty insisting they turn back before it got dark.

In the background, something white stepped out from behind a tree, then disappeared. It couldn't have lasted more than a half second.

I heard myself gasp.

Didi paused the video. "Weird, huh?"

"What was it? It went by too fast."

"That's because it's just a few frames long. I'll slow it down."

My heart was pounding while Didi rewound the video and played it back, frame by frame. I could make out the figure more clearly.

It was a man with a very white face, dressed in dark clothes, a hood covering his head. He was slightly stooped, with unusually long arms. What chilled me was the face. It appeared to be made of bits of torn paper, eyes drooping and uneven. It was the same one I had seen in the gully after Misty Denner's death.

And while I watched, one frame at a time, it slid out of view.

Didi rewound the video and stopped it on the figure. He was staring directly at Misty, as if transfixed.

"Shit," I said.

"That was *exactly* my reaction." Didi dragged her hands through her hair and succeeded in pulling her glasses off her face. "Everyone swears they'd never seen it before. No one noticed it while they were shooting. I only saw it this morning as I was logging the footage."

Hairs lifted on the back of my neck. "Is it possible someone messed with the film? Did a little trick photography or something?" I knew the answer, but I had to ask.

"No." Didi picked up her glasses from her lap and stuck them back on her nose. "No way. This is raw footage. No special effects have been added yet. Which is why I think it must be a prank. But considering what happened to Misty and Naomi, I don't like it."

My hands had begun to cramp. When I glanced down, I was clutching the arms of the chair. I released my hold and wriggled my aching fingers. "Wasn't Naomi the director of photography? Did she shoot that footage?"

Didi nodded, frowning. "She did. But she never said anything about it. She was probably so focused on the talent that she didn't notice. Naomi was super intense when she was working. Which made her so good at what she did."

I dragged my eyes back to the screen, at that horrible white face. "And no one else saw it either? Don't people look at the film after it's shot?"

"Sometimes, they'll screen the footage at the end of the day, but right after they shot this scene, the camera rig slipped, and Naomi fell. She wasn't badly hurt, but there was some panic about the whole thing. Naomi was worried about the camera, so she fussed with it for a while, apparently. Anyway, I was the first one to see the footage when I got in this morning."

"Does that face look like it's got makeup on it?" I asked.

Didi glanced at me like I was an idiot. "Um, yeah. What else could it be?"

I had some ideas, but my mind often went places normal people's didn't, so I kept my mouth shut. "I don't know. Just out of curiosity, what do the producers plan on doing with that scene?"

"They have several takes, but I'm sure they'll make the most out of that one," she said flatly. "It'll give them something to talk about during the press tour. Which is what makes me think someone on the crew staged it." She paused. "But if they did, a makeup artist would have been involved, and ours wasn't. He's my husband, and he was as surprised as the rest of us when he saw that clip."

This had been a much more interesting meeting than I had expected, but I had arrived with questions, and I needed to get them answered.

"Did Naomi ever say anything about the production being cursed?"

"Oh, yeah. She loved it," Didi said with a sad smile. "She was a huge horror fan, so it was just the kind of thing she *would* love. And she was no dummy. She could see the marketing potential."

"Were they friends? Misty and Naomi?"

Didi shook her head. "Friendly, I'd say, but not friends. The only thing those two seemed to have in common was their height. They were both tiny things."

"How tall was Naomi?"

"She couldn't be more than five feet, maybe five foot one?"

Interesting. The two victims had been short, whatever that meant.

Didi's knee was bouncing up and down, and her eyes kept drifting to the screens on her desk.

"I'm almost done, I promise," I said. "Has the detective from the LAPD talked to anyone working on the film?"

Didi tapped her mouth, her fingers fluttering against her lips. "Kind of. With some of the crew. Certainly not with me. She called a meeting in the commissary and asked the producers and actors to call her if they knew anything that could be relevant. Handed out a phone number. But that was it. Not exactly a grilling."

"Last question, I swear. Do you know if anyone on the crew called that number after they saw that…thing in the trees?"

Didi shook her head. "I seriously doubt it. The director told everyone to keep quiet about it. They didn't want it leaking before the press tour." Didi jutted her chin out, and her dark eyes glittered behind the glasses. "I guess I'm not very good at following orders, 'cause here I am, talking to you." She smirked.

I pointed at the screen. "Is it okay if I take a pic? Just for my files. I'm not a big sharer."

She hesitated so long I was sure she would refuse. "Okay," she finally said. "But just don't tell anyone where you got it, or I could lose my job."

"Understood." I grabbed the photo before she could change her mind.

When I got up to leave, I decided to push my luck with one more question.

"Is it possible to know exactly where this was shot?"

Didi sighed. "I'll find out. Give me your number and I'll text you when I know. But now, I really need to get back to work."

"I appreciate your help here. And I'm really leaving this time, I mean it."

Didi waved and spun her chair back to her desk.

My mind was racing with possibilities. It now seemed likely the mysterious figure in the film was connected to the deaths of Misty Denner and Naomi Taylor. Which was why he had been in the gully the night of Misty's murder.

I made my way down the dark hallway and out of the decrepit building.

It felt good to be back in the harsh sunlight of the real world.

Chapter 23

Ron sent me a steady stream of nerd sightings while Steve and his OA research buddies looked for signs of entity 2.0 entry points. Steve had promised to alert me to anything important, and I trusted he would. Still, I was glad to have eyes on the group because one never could be too cautious. The nerds were sometimes a sneaky bunch.

After my visit to the production company, I called a brief team meeting in the command center. We were in the middle of home safety audits, so not everyone could make it, but I needed to bring my team up to speed on my conversation with the film editor.

While Liam, Justin, Brandon, and Ron settled into their chairs, I quickly explained what I had learned, then held out my phone and showed them the pic I had taken of the figure in the grove.

"What the hell?" Justin gasped.

Ron blinked rapidly. "Is that what you saw in the gully?"

"That looks like Lon Chaney in *Phantom of the Opera*. Except for the skin, of course," Liam said. "And maybe the teeth. Hard to tell with its mouth closed."

I laughed. "Thank you, Roger Ebert. I hadn't figured you for a film scholar, Liam. Yes, that looks just like the guy I saw the night of Misty's murder."

Brandon cracked his knuckles. "Boss, if you saw it in La Loma and this same thing was sneaking around the set where our victims were working, it's got to be him. *Whatever* he is."

"Can I see your phone?" Liam asked. "I want to check something."

Liam enlarged the image and squinted at the screen.

"Could be someone wearing really good special effects makeup. What did your source think?"

"That's exactly what she thought," I said, plucking my phone from Liam's plate-sized hand. "She just assumed it was makeup. Which makes sense, given where she works."

Liam snorted. "We've had some pretty scary-looking entities. You'd think they'd be more open to other possibilities."

Justin shuddered. "The way it's looking at Misty Denner…"

"How long was that thing in the shot?" Liam asked.

"Just a few frames. And there's something else. They found hairs under Naomi's nails. The lab says they're neither human nor animal. Which means we could be dealing with something totally new."

Justin and Liam exchanged looks.

"Well, one thing's for sure," Justin said. "Things never get boring around here."

Ron leaned forward, eyes narrowed. "So, what's our next move, boss?"

I took a moment to gather my thoughts. That was a great question. And I didn't have a great answer.

My phone chimed. A message from Didi.

"Perfect timing. My source just sent over the exact location of the shoot in Phantom's Pass. It's possible we'll find more clues there and, if we're lucky, maybe even discover where this thing is hiding out. You guys coordinate a search, but please be careful and be discrete. We don't know what we're dealing with, and we don't want Bevlov accusing us of getting in her way."

While Justin and Liam huddled together over a map, I walked across Palo Verde Plaza to my office. Sitting in my chair, I stared at the mysterious image on my phone once more.

I had encountered a few ghouls before. They were bad enough. But there was something about that pale figure that sent a chill down my spine.

I tucked the phone back in my pocket.

Bailey was one of the best, and she was the only one I trusted to walk our nervous residents through their home security reviews. But I felt a little guilty for heaping all that responsibility on her shoulders, so I joined her for the walkthroughs she had scheduled that afternoon.

The women we met were more interested in asking questions about the police investigation—questions we couldn't answer—than they were in the safety tips we shared. Not that I blamed them. It was a scary time. But Bailey skillfully focused them on our safety recommendations, and when we left, they were noticeably calmer.

The afternoon dragged on until, finally, we took a quick break at Muertos Café. Bailey and I sat on the cool patio, sipping our iced coffees, and I caught her up on the information I had shared with the others earlier.

Bailey clutched her glass and gave a weary sigh. "We've dealt with serious stuff before, but never murder. And with all the cameras we have around here, how has this person—or whatever—not been caught on video? That thing you showed me isn't a ghost."

I leaned back in my chair. The late afternoon sun cast our table in shadow.

"You're right. If a film camera can capture it, our security cameras can too. But they haven't, which means it knows how to evade them."

"That doesn't sound like an entity." Bailey twisted a lock of copper hair around a finger.

"No," I agreed. "No, it doesn't. At least, not the kind we've dealt with so far."

Bailey groaned and dragged her hands down her face. Somehow, her blue eyeshadow did not smear. "I don't know if I'm ready to deal with new entities."

Neither was I. But we might not have had a choice.

After our break and another couple of hours in the office, I decided it was time to call it quits, go home, and let the cat out. Sam had a litter box, but he preferred to do his business outside, like a dog. I made a quick stop at the market in Palo Verde and bought the makings for grilled shrimp salad with avocado.

Just as I had started up the Jeep, my cell phone rang. It was Ben Tomas.

I picked up immediately. "Everything all right?"

"No. One of my guys says he saw something. Someone getting attacked."

My heart jumped into my throat. "Did you call the police?"

"No. He begged me not to call them. He's afraid of the police. So, I'm calling you."

"Ben, if someone's being attacked, we need to call the police and an ambulance right now."

"Maddy, I'm there now, and I don't think there's anything an ambulance can do."

There was no time to waste. No time to interrogate Ben about what had happened.

"Just send me the address and I'll get there as fast as I can. And Ben, don't touch anything."

I drove to the address in Bishop as fast as I dared, finding myself in one of Chavez Ravine's most peculiar areas.

Bishop Circles was a newer development across from Bad Pete's compound. It backed up onto Phantom's Pass. I didn't know what genius had decided to build a neighborhood laid out in concentric circles, but I cursed them when I made a wrong turn and got stuck in a maze of one-way streets.

Finally, after violating several driving laws, I pulled up to the house—a large Spanish-style affair complete with cream-colored stucco, brown trim, and wooden balconies. Minimal but lovely landscaping. There were two white trucks parked in the street and an expensive-looking black SUV with tinted windows in the driveway.

Ben jogged over to meet me. Before I could say a word, he pointed at a palm tree. Brown fronds lay scattered on the ground.

"Felipe was up there when he saw it. I'm not able to make much sense of his story, but whatever he saw scared the hell out of him."

"Where's the body?"

Ben pointed at the yard next to the palm tree, and I took off.

I ran through the front lawn, then turned right into the bordering yard. On one side, the house rose two stories, with large windows and a balcony outside a bedroom. On the other side of the yard, at the property line, was a motionless figure crumpled against a stucco wall.

I was there in seconds, kneeling and feeling for a pulse, but I was much too late.

After getting to my feet, I took a good look at the body. A young man, maybe early thirties. He appeared to be in good shape but had still been no match for whatever had attacked him. And bitten him on the legs.

Another tragedy. Another meaningless death. Another shock for the residents of Chavez Ravine.

I was beginning to take this personally.

Ben was waiting when I returned to the street.

"Have you seen any of the neighbors?"

Ben shook his head. "No. I know the people here, and most of them are probably still at work. The family next door is on vacation."

"Okay. I'll have a quick chat with your guy, but then I'll have to call the police."

Ben grimaced. "He's going to freak out. I'm just warning you."

"What's the problem? Is he illegal?"

Ben stepped back and blew out a noisy breath. "No. I don't hire illegals. Even if I wanted to, the board would never allow it. It's just that his English has never been very good."

I nodded, then followed Ben toward the truck and the man waiting by the passenger side. He had brown skin, a bald head, and an impressive barrel chest.

"This is Felipe Contreras. He's worked for me for coming up on two years." Ben continued in Spanish. "Felipe, this is Maddy Madrigal. She's in charge of security. I know you don't want to talk to the police, but you have to tell her what you saw." Ben turned to me. "How's your Spanish? Do you need me to translate?"

I glanced at the safety gear heaped on the patch of grass near Felipe's feet. "I'm far from fluent, but I think we can get by. You can always jump in."

Felipe eyed me warily. "I didn't see much."

The man was obviously nervous. If I wanted him to talk, I would have to take it slowly and in steps. "You were trimming the palm tree?"

"Yes."

"Did you use a ladder, or did you climb it?"

The man's chest puffed out a little. "I don't need a ladder. I climb them. All the way to the top. I cut down the palm tree in your backyard."

"Did you? You did a very good job, thank you." I smiled, then glanced over at the house. If Felipe had been near the top, he would have had a straight line of sight to the second story. "So, you were cutting down those big fronds, and then what happened?"

The man covered his face with his hands, which were calloused and worn. "It was terrible. I don't want to say it."

"Felipe," I said sternly. "There's someone dead in the yard, and you saw what happened. You are a very important witness. I'm going to be honest with you. You need to tell me what you saw, and then you're going to need to tell the police."

"No!" he shouted. "Not the police. They won't believe me."

I took a few deep breaths, trying to stay calm. "*I* will believe you, Felipe. No matter what you say. But you need to tell me what happened."

Tears flooded his eyes. He crossed himself. Not once, but several times. "The man who lives in the house was in that room, lifting and stuff."

That got my attention. "Lifting? Like, exercising?"

"Yes. He's very small. Like a boy. But he drives that big car, and he's strong. He was lifting when I was in the palm tree."

Felipe paused and wiped his eyes with the back of his hand.

"And then what happened?" I prompted.

"The man came to the window and waved, and he turned around. I thought he was coming down to give me a tip."

He glanced at Ben, then back to me.

"We're not supposed to take tips, but it's hard to say no. And then I saw someone standing right behind him, and the man screamed. And then he was flying out of the window and across the yard and hit the wall near the trees. And then the other guy jumped out the window and ran over to him, and I heard more screaming, and it was terrible. I started to yell. To tell that pinche cabron to stop, but he didn't."

Felipe rubbed his eyes with his hands, struggling to control his breathing.

"I climbed down as fast as I could. I grabbed a saw and ran to the side of the house. Then that guy saw me and ran away..." His voice trailed off.

"What did he look like?" I couldn't keep the eagerness out of my voice.

Felipe turned away, refusing to meet my eyes.

"You need to tell me." I placed a gentle hand on his shoulder.

Felipe whipped his head toward me, his eyes round, nearly wild. "No!"

The man shut down. That was all I was going to get. I turned to Ben with a sigh.

"Any idea what's going on here?"

Ben nodded slowly. "Yes." He spoke in a low voice. "He said it was El Cucuy."

My eyes seemed to have a life of their own, blinking and bugging out. "The Cucuy?"

Felipe cried out and crossed himself again. "I said you wouldn't believe me!"

The sun was setting, the hottest part of a long day. A trickle of sweat ran down my back.

El Cucuy, the boogeyman of childhood nightmares. It seemed impossible, but the fear in Felipe's eyes was real.

143

"I know what I saw," Felipe said through gritted teeth. "El Cucuy is here."

Chapter 24

Felipe asked that I be present during the interview, and to my surprise, Bevlov agreed. To my even greater shock, she was gentle with the gardener while he spoke in low, worried tones to the young translator.

I swept my hair into a bun with a scrunchie, longing for a cold drink.

Felipe's hands trembled slightly when he recounted his story. The translator, Valentina, spoke softly and repeated Felipe's story to Detective Bevlov.

Bevlov's steady gaze never left the gardener's face. When she asked him to describe the attacker he had seen through the window, he flicked his eyes toward me, and then his features hardened into a mask. He said he had seen a man dressed in dark clothes, a hood covering his head, but only for a second. Not long enough to get a good look at his face, but he was very pale, nearly white.

Bevlov frowned. Felipe's hands fidgeted in his lap. She pushed harder for more details, and I held my breath. If Felipe mentioned El Cucuy, his credibility would be shot, and he would probably become a suspect.

But the man shook his head and stuck to his story.

Finally, after what felt like an eternity, the interview was over.

Bevlov pulled me aside. Her eyes narrowed. "Did he tell you anything different than he told us?"

"No." Not for the first time, I was a little amazed at how easy it was to lie. At least to certain people under certain circumstances.

"Is that right?" Her voice dripped with sarcasm.

I gave a little shrug. "How's Cooper? Do you still have him?"

"Cooper is with his grandparents in Sherman Oaks," Bevlov said stiffly. "I'll be having a word with the gardener. It's unacceptable he called you before us."

"He's a master landscaper," I corrected automatically. "And please, give him a break. People here aren't used to calling the police. That's why the association has its own security team."

Bevlov flinched.

Oops. I had just become a walking, breathing reminder she had blown the job she had tried so hard to get.

"Hasn't done them much good, has it?" she said coldly, then strode off to the side of the house to join the medical examiner.

I watched her go, wishing I could tag along. It was my suspicion the killer had been trying to drag the victim into the woods when Felipe came tearing around the corner with his saw. It would have been nice to have the M.E. confirm that theory.

A few moments later, Bevlov reappeared.

"I'm sure you have something important to do, like hunting down unauthorized lawn ornaments or kissing board members' asses, so be on your way."

I shrugged. "Your circus, your monkeys." It was a silly thing to say, but it felt good.

Besides, I really did have plenty to keep me busy.

Halfway down the hill, I pulled over and called Ron in the command center. "How's that search going in Phantom's Pass? Anything yet?"

"Nothing so far, boss. But that's not too surprising. I've been hiking there since I was a kid. It's bigger than you'd think and pretty wild in parts."

I filled him in on the latest murder and Felipe's theory about who had done it.

Ron gave a low whistle. "He saw the Cucuy? Oh man. I knew it. I knew he'd surface someday."

I sighed. "Ron, the witness *said* he saw El Cucuy. We don't know what he *really* saw. And Ron, you know the Cucuy is just a story meant to scare kids into behaving, right?"

Ron snorted loudly. "The Chupacabra was just supposed to be a story, but one of those fuckers bit me."

He had a point. All the entities that had appeared in Los Angeles had once been legends or myths or stories too. And if the thing I had seen in the gully and on the film footage wasn't El Cucuy, what was it?

"Okay, you've got a good point." I felt deflated and overwhelmed. "Can you please radio the team searching in Phantom's Pass? They need to know this thing has struck again and it's dangerous. Please remind them to be very, very careful out there."

"Will do, boss."

We hung up, and I called Cora to give her the bad news.

"That's not far from my house!" she cried. "I need to tell my daughters not to bring the babies over. Not until the killer is caught." She paused. "I guess we should send an alert."

I cleared my throat. "Yes, that's a good idea. Cora, I'm going to tell you something, but you need to keep this to yourself. There's no reason to cause more panic than there already is. Promise?"

"Madre mia de Dios!" Cora's voice was barely above a whisper. "Yes, I promise."

"There was a witness. One of Ben's guys. He saw the murderer, and he swears it was El Cucuy."

Cora gasped. When she finally spoke, her voice was hushed. "My mother said he used to come around. A long time ago. Before the city tried to kick everyone out. There were stories about him taking children away. Things got so bad that the people got together and asked your great-aunt Lencha to do something, so she made a spell to keep him out."

I was parked on the side of the road near a short two-way bridge that spanned the gully. A group of women dressed in workout clothes power-walked past my Jeep, arms swinging—out for an early evening stroll. Safety in numbers.

They peered inside, and I gave a friendly wave in return. Relieved to see a woman, they returned the gesture and hurried across the bridge.

"I guess that spell isn't working anymore," I said. "If it really is the Cucuy, I mean."

Cora let out a shaky breath. "There's more to that story. A young lady who lived in La Loma had a little boy who used to act up, as kids do. But she got so frustrated she tried to scare him by calling for the Cucuy to come and take him away. And he did."

I pressed a finger between my eyes. "Oh, no. Let me guess. When she invited him in, she broke Lencha's spell?"

"That's exactly what my mother said. It's an awful story, really. I used to think she made it up just to scare me. She said the Cucuy came and took the little boy away, and the mother had to pay a terrible price to get her little boy back."

I swallowed hard. "That *is* an awful story."

The thing was, I also believed it. Considering everything else that had happened since I took this crazy job, the Cucuy was the most likely explanation.

"I need to find out more about El Cucuy. Any idea who I can talk to?"

Cora didn't hesitate. "Hernan Frias. If anyone knows anything, it's him, with his teaching background."

Of course. "Thanks, Cora. I've got a team searching Phantom's Pass. If El Cucuy is out there, they may be able to find some evidence."

When we hung up, I drove straight to Muertos Café and bought three dinner specials to-go. I couldn't expect help from Hernan without a bribe.

Chapter 25

Marta, Hernan's caretaker, set plates and silverware on a small table in the corner of Hernan's home library. We sat down, surrounded by towering bookshelves packed with volumes on Mexican folklore, history, and mysticism. Like most of the house, the room had dark, heavy wooden furniture. Maroon velvet drapes covered the windows, and the air was stale. By the state of his cluttered desk, it appeared Hernan had spent a lot of time in there.

In these strange, uncomfortable surroundings, I felt disconnected from my life. From Stu. From my cat. From my herb garden and my kitchen stocked with food I hadn't had the time or energy to prepare. I hadn't even checked with Clare to see how things had turned out at her soccer game.

But duty called.

Without bothering to ask, I got up, pushed aside the curtains, and opened the window. The air that poured in was warm, but at least it was fresh.

Hernan sputtered in protest, but I ignored him. Marta shot me a nervous smile, then slipped away to enjoy a rare meal in peace, leaving me to handle her difficult charge for a while.

The retired professor dug into his chicken mole. Between mouthfuls, he said, "I got that alert. It was another murder, wasn't it?"

The mention of death should have been enough to put me off my food, but I was starving. I eyed my plate hungrily. The enticing aroma of chili, chocolate, and a hint of cinnamon wafted through the room. I tore off a piece of flour tortilla and scooped up some tender chicken bathed in the rich sauce.

"Unfortunately, it was," I said.

"This is just a wild guess on my part, but I think you want something from me." Hernan raised his dark eyebrows. "Do you?"

"Just your expertise." I wasn't above a little flattery. It had worked before.

Hernan dabbed his mouth with a napkin. "What is it this time?"

"What can you tell me about El Cucuy?"

Hernan scowled. "The Cucuy?" he said, his voice rising. "Are you serious? What do you…why would you…"

"I'm dead serious."

Hernan sat straighter in his chair. "Let's hear it. And no pussyfooting around."

I leaned forward. "What I'm about to say can't leave this room. Do you agree?" When Hernan nodded, I continued. "The person who witnessed the crime says the attacker was El Cucuy. He was terrified. I have reasons to believe he may be right. Do you think it's possible?"

Hernan shrugged. "He's like any legend. There's never been any real proof." He pointed at a framed print on the wall. "That's an etching by Goya. It's called *Que Viene el Coco*. Here comes the boogeyman."

I stared at the print. It showed a cowering woman holding two crying, terrified children—a little on the gloomy side for my taste.

"I won't go into all the theories about what he's supposed to represent, but what you should know is our Cucuy goes way back, and he goes by other names in other places. Cuco. Cuca. The Cucuy. The Coco Man."

"Where does the name come from?"

"Probably from the word *coconut*. Some people described the boogeyman as a hairy monster, and since the coconut is hairy, well, you can see how that got started. He probably comes from medieval Spain and Portugal. Some scholars link Coco to a Portuguese ghost with a jack-o'-lantern head who used to go around, scaring children.

"The thing is, our El Cucuy takes many forms, but the stories about him have one thing in common: he steals misbehaving children and takes them to his lair, where he eats them. Slowly." Hernan gave a dismissive sniff. "This can't be the Cucuy. Not if he's killing adults."

Yeah, I'd thought about that too.

Hernan launched into more detail than I had thought possible, and my mind drifted, trying to grasp onto a fleeting idea, a thought that was both elusive and persistent.

I snapped out of it when Hernan started talking about the Cucuy stalking Chavez Ravine and a bargain my great-aunt had struck with the creature. But he dismissed the story, as he did much of the lore surrounding Lencha. Apparently, jealousy and resentment had been passed down from one generation to another in the Frias family.

Marta brought in two bottles of Mexican beer and two glasses. Hernan popped off the tops and poured.

I took a couple of thirsty gulps. "Does the Cucuy have any weaknesses?"

"You mean, like wooden stakes and vampires?"

"Yes. Because, if we're dealing with the Cucuy, it would be nice to know if there's a handy way to kill him."

Hernan shook his head. "I've never come across anything like that." He jerked a thumb at a bookshelf behind him. "I have a couple of books back there that might mention it. I can take a look, if you'd like. There's also a fellow in Mexico I could call and ask."

I nearly choked on my beer. It dribbled out of my mouth. Was Hernan offering to *help*?

"That would be great, thank you."

Hernan scowled and slid a fresh napkin across the table. "Have you thought about using the powers that have been inexplicably granted you? The famous Lencha could have figured it out, surely."

His voice dripped with sarcasm. Like my mother, Hernan seemed to resent the boost I had gotten from my great-aunt. Neither missed an opportunity to remind me I hadn't put in enough work to earn my bruja status, iffy as it was.

I dabbed my mouth and sighed. "I have no idea how to do that."

"You might be able to if—"

"If I hadn't skipped the line. I know, I know." I got to my feet before Hernan could lecture me some more. "If you learn anything, would you please call me immediately?"

Hernan raised his hand and shooed me away. "Yes, yes. Now go on. Leave me alone so I can do your homework for you."

No way to treat a lady who brings you food, if you ask me.

I said goodbye to Marta and left through the front door. The evening air was as warm and thick as soup. While I drove through the quiet neighborhoods, my conversation with Felipe played over in my head. The man had been truly frightened, and not just because of the police. Could it really have been El Cucuy haunting the streets of Chavez Ravine?

I knew just who to ask.

Chapter 26

I came home to my cat grooming himself on his favorite ottoman. He glanced in my direction, blinked his green eyes a few times, then went back to licking between his toes. My neighbor, Leo, had dropped by earlier to feed Sam. He had texted he had helped himself to a glass of wine and sat out back, enjoying the patio.

And that's the only reason Sam wasn't yelling at me for being gone for so long; Leo was one of his favorite humans.

"Traitor," I said, flicking on my new air conditioning unit.

Sam ignored me. Two could play that game. I walked past him toward the sunroom.

Little Lencha sat quietly on the wooden bench. The clay eyes that often tracked my movements showed no interest while I stood before her. I wondered what it must take for her spirit to appear. Was it only when I really needed her? When she had a solution to one of my problems? Then now would have been a good time to show up.

Maybe my great-aunt was tired of helping me. Maybe she just wanted me to get on with things on my own and let her rest. Or maybe she was waiting for me to start the conversation.

I lit a vanilla-scented candle and began pacing in front of my workbench. "So, Tia, I've heard that story about you banishing El Cucuy from Chavez Ravine. But someone goofed up your spell, and he came back. Is that true?"

I stared at the figurine, anticipating.

Nothing.

"Just talking things through here. Maybe that old story is true, or your Cucuy spell has worn out. Or maybe the Cucuy has figured out a way around it. Whichever, I'd appreciate it if you could give me some pointers so I can get the spell back up." I paused, waiting for the figurine to illuminate. "Feel free to throw a girl a bone here."

Still nothing, although Sam sauntered in, probably wondering who I was talking to.

"Okay. Maybe you don't like dwelling in the past. I get that. I've got things in my past I don't like talking about either, though most of *them* have names, like Greg. But you did warn me about something, so if that something was El Cucuy, then it would be great if you could add just a tad bit more information."

Without moving, the small clay figure managed to appear bored out of her mind.

A knock on the door put a quick end to my interrogation of Little Lencha. It was Clare, alone this time.

My heart sank. "You shouldn't be in Chavez Ravine," I said sternly. "Not with everything going on. Your dad would not be happy if he knew you were here."

Clare scraped a hand through her dark hair. "I know, I'm sorry. But I had no place else to go. My mom and I had a fight, and I needed to get away. She's driving me crazy. Please, can I come in?"

I pulled her inside and gave her a hug. She rested her head on my shoulder and sniffled.

"I won't stay long, I promise."

My to-do list would have to wait a few minutes.

I had never had to cheer up a teenage girl before. While I had been a pretty moody one myself, my mother had always left me to figure things out on my own. Not the greatest role model, I know.

And then, inspiration struck.

"Want to make some ice cream?" I asked.

Clare smiled. "Really? I've never made it before! Is it hard?"

"I don't know. I haven't made it either, but it can't be any harder than making mole sauce from scratch."

I pulled out the base of the ice cream maker from the pantry and the chilled bowl from the freezer, then walked Clare through the steps to make a simple syrup. While it cooled, we squeezed fresh lemons and grated the zest.

I added salt to the mixture and gave it a taste. "It's too sweet. What if we added a bit of chili to spice it up?"

Clare grinned. "Really? All right. That sounds good."

"It's worth trying." I showed Clare how to seed the small red chilis, which we threw into a blender with a bit of water.

"It's a pretty color," Clare said, peering into the bowl.

Our concoction was the shade of a sunset. Clare scraped it into the pre-frozen bowl, and moments later, our sorbet was churning away. I made us yerba buena tea, which we drank in the living room.

"My dad says he misses us. Like you *and* me," Clare said.

Butterflies danced in my stomach. "Did he?"

"He did. I talked to him this morning. He said he's having fun with my uncle and the guys, but he can't wait to come home."

"That's nice." It felt a little weird to hear that from his daughter rather than Stu himself. *When had we last talked?* I was losing track of time.

"Yeah. It's weird him not being here. He said that if I was having a tough time with anything, I could talk to you."

"And are you?" I asked lightly. "Having a tough time with anything?"

Clare stared down into her mug. "Yeah. You know that thing you made our friend? That ankle wrap? It worked. Like, really,

really worked. We went to my mom's house and put it on. It didn't smell great, but our goalie woke up the next morning feeling fine, and she played better than ever. She stopped three penalty kicks! Not a single goal got past her. We won four-zero!"

How about that? My remedy had worked, and at lightning speed. So why did Clare seem so stricken?

"Congratulations! For the record, my remedy only fixed her ankle. The talent was all hers. So, Clare, what's wrong?"

"My mom found the jar with the leftover stuff you made. She asked what it was, and I told her, but I didn't expect her to freak out like she did. So, I kind of told her that you were into Mexican healing arts and that it was something to fix a sprained ankle, and she just sort of lost it."

The confession left Clare breathless.

Great. Clare had given her mother every reason to think I was nuts.

Clare's phone rang, and we both jumped.

She stared at the screen, her eyes going wide. "Oh crap. It's my mom."

"Maybe she just wants to make sure you're okay."

Clare cast a doubtful glance in my direction. "Hi, Mom. What's up?" Her voice was flatter than a tortilla.

The woman wasn't even on speaker, and I could make her out clearly. I distinctly heard the word *bitch* more than once. After my long, tiring, and frustrating day, that was the last thing I needed.

"Uh huh, uh huh, uh huh," Clare said, then handed me the phone. "She wants to talk to you."

Time to pull on the Big Girl Panties. I cleared my throat. "This is Maddy Madrigal," I said briskly.

Vicki Wells unleashed a tirade. "How dare you try to draw my daughter into your freaky devil-worshiping cult! That stuff reeked! You really crossed the line here. She's a minor, and I do not like the weird influence you seem to have over her. And don't think I haven't heard about those protection amulets—or whatever they're supposed to be. No normal adult would try to lure a child with that brew-ha-whatever you do."

"Brujería?" I offered.

"Whatever it is, you can keep it to yourself. I don't want you spending any more time with my daughter, and I'm going to make that clear to Stu, whenever he decides he's had enough partying in Vegas."

Throughout her tirade, I imagined myself zipped in a giant plastic bag, unable to hear anything from the outside world. It was a skill I had perfected every time the chief of Occult Affairs droned on.

Clare stared at me, clearly horrified.

"I'll send Clare home," I said stiffly.

"You do that! And adios, Señora Madrigal." The way she said it—slowly, mispronouncing each syllable—made me want to throw the phone across the room.

After I ended the call, Clare's shoulders slumped. "I'm sorry. About my mom. If I hadn't come, she wouldn't have yelled at you like that. That was really mean."

I walked Clare to the door and ruffled her hair. "You're not responsible for your mother's behavior."

After I had escorted Clare to her SUV parked in the driveway, she turned a bleary-eyed face toward me. "I wish I could stay with you," she said, then drove away.

Clare might have wished for something else if she had known I was the reason her father left town.

Chapter 27

The next morning, I woke early, did a full-body workout with weights, then took a quick shower, pulled on some clothes and my gold trench coat, and headed for the office.

Just as I was foaming milk for a latte on the fancy coffee machine I had fallen in love with, my phone chimed. Bevlov had issued a press release announcing a new homicide investigation was underway in the Bishop neighborhood of Chavez Ravine.

The victim, identified as Brad Plante, thirty-five, had been found unresponsive outside his home on the 1300 block of Bishop Circle. The preliminary investigation indicated Mr. Plante had sustained a broken neck.

Motive unclear, etc., etc. Detectives working diligently, as though there was another way to work. Bevlov needed a creative writing class.

But the release got more interesting toward the end.

Mr. Plante had spent fifteen years in the film industry. He had worked on a number of successful independent pictures, most of them horror films.

The suspect in his death was described as a Caucasian male of undetermined age, approximately six feet tall, with a hunched back and thin build. He was wearing a dark hoodie and dark pants. No mention of his pale face or paper-mâché skin.

Anyone with information about the suspect or the incident was advised to call Steven Zhao. The release included his telephone number and email address.

Poor Steve.

I turned on my computer and watched my inbox fill up in real time. Residents were scared and angry. I checked in with Ron in the command center, and he said they were getting overwhelmed with complaints on the emergency number. Some of them had been quite rude, he said.

I dialed Cora. The board was being flooded with angry emails from residents asking why it was spending so much money on a security team who couldn't protect them from a killer.

Not all that long ago, I had been heralded as a hero for taking out some monster birds with a slingshot at Pete Drury's place. But now, I was a slacker who couldn't have been bothered to do my job.

I couldn't exactly issue my own press release indicating we suspected the Cucuy. But Cora was sympathetic. She was going to draft a response we could use to respond to our angry callers.

I called Didi, the editor on *Phantom's Pass*. She picked up immediately. Spooky music blared in the background.

"I was wondering when I'd hear from you," she said.

"Was Brad Plante involved with *Phantom's Pass*?"

"That he was." Didi exhaled loudly. "He was one of our producers. Though, he was pretty hands-on for a producer. Probably because he started off as a production assistant and worked his way up. He was there that day in Phantom's Pass, where they caught that weird guy on film."

"Did you know Brad well?" I asked.

"Not really. But he seemed to be a nice guy. People who knew him genuinely liked him. Even though he was short, he wasn't a dick. There are plenty of those in this business. I actually heard someone call him 'fun-sized' to his face once. He just laughed it off. Plenty of people would pull that 'you'll never work in this town again' routine."

I thanked Didi and hung up. A sense of unease settled in the pit of my stomach.

Three murder victims, three members of the *Phantom's Pass* crew, three strikes against the head of security for Chavez Ravine.

The more I turned the facts over in my head, the more convinced I was El Cucuy was our killer. Too many things fit: the humanoid bitemarks, the foul odor, the skulking around in the gully, the strength to fling a man out a window and across the yard. There were still a couple of open questions, such as why he was attacking adults and not kidnapping children, like the legendary boogeyman. We needed to figure that out.

But deciding he was our bad guy was only half a solution. Knowing how to take him out was the other, and I was miles away from that.

Eventually, I would need to conjure something that would dispose of El Cucuy, but before I could do that, I needed to know what Lencha had done to banish him all those years ago, and I had to learn more about his history and vulnerabilities. Perhaps Hernan Frias would turn up something useful, but I couldn't bank on it.

I needed someone who could gaze into the past, who could try to get inside the Cucuy's head and find his weaknesses.

There seemed to be only one option, and I hated that feeling.

But desperate times and desperate measures and all that.

I finished my latte, took a deep breath, and called my mother.

Chapter 28

Nothing about my mother was easy. When we spoke, it was hard to follow her elliptical thoughts. When I visited her, it took all my strength to ignore the barbs. And when we went anywhere together, I had to pick her up because she didn't drive.

Gnome-infested Beverly Hills was a mess. Abandoned homes, empty streets, boarded-up shops. The only nice thing about the community was the landscaping, and that was thanks to the industrious gnomes that had taken over.

At my mother's place, her cadre of gnomes had transformed the front yard, and it now resembled an English country garden. I had liked it better the old way, with the native grasses and succulents, but it was obvious my mother had lost that battle. There was no arguing with gnomes once they moved in, even if one was the famous entity whisperer, Malena Bantacorte.

When I pulled into the driveway, I noticed several working on a garden trellis. They stopped and stared at me with their dark, beady eyes. Straw hats protected their sensitive grayish-green skin from the Southern California sun.

Occult Affairs categorized them as entities because they had appeared shortly after the first big earthquake, but they didn't behave like the others. They shook off their confusion almost immediately, and Smoke Bombs didn't sedate them for very long. Carting them off to The Dump was a waste of time. They always escaped and found their way back to the west side of Los Angeles.

Before my mother bought her house at an unheard-of price, the gnomes had taken over the yards, refused to share the outdoor spaces with the owners, and terrorized the dogs. They *hated* canines. But my mother had quickly sorted all that out.

She had assigned gnomes to houses so they were more evenly distributed throughout the city and even got them to allow dogs in the backyards long enough to do their business. That's all it had taken for my mother to become a hero in Beverly Hills. She even had a park named after her.

One of the gnomes hopped off a ladder and waddled toward the Jeep.

"Go away," I muttered. I wasn't in the mood to deal with any of their shenanigans.

My mother knew I was in a hurry. If I went inside, she would start puttering around, showing me things and telling stories, and we would never get out of there. I honked the horn.

The gnome stared, eyes boring into me. I could take him if I had to, even without a pouch, but I wasn't in the mood.

"Shoo," I said through the open window.

He kept staring.

I felt dizzy, and my vision blurred. Panic gripped me. Was I having some sort of medical episode? I touched my face to make sure I could still feel it, then counted to ten and moved my feet up and down in the footwell.

The gnome and I locked eyes. And then I was speeding through a tunnel, tumbling through the darkness, emerging into the light, watching a group of gnomes running toward me through a brilliant green valley.

Something huge was chasing them.

A shadow.

Something I couldn't see in the sky above.

Their little faces twisted in fear, and then a hole appeared in the ground, and they threw themselves down it, disappearing.

My vision cleared. The gnome was gone, and my mother was climbing into the Jeep. My heart pounded.

What the hell was that?

I turned my head toward the passenger seat, hardly recognizing my mother. She wore an animal print scarf over her auburn hair. Oversized dark glasses, white jeans, and an orange blouse completed the picture, like she was going sailing on the bay with the Kennedys.

I had never thought I would say this, but I missed the shapeless caftans.

"Look at you," I said.

My mother turned in her seat and frowned. "Look at *you*. Or should I say, look what the cat dragged in."

Here we go.

Though, she had a point. I hadn't bothered to fix my hair or put on makeup, which was very unlike me. But given everything that was going on, I forgave myself.

My mother, on the other hand, didn't.

"You know, at your age, Madeline, one must make more of an effort."

Deep breath. It's only a few hours.

She yanked at the seatbelt and struggled to pull it across her lap.

I leaned over her, grabbed the metal end with unsteady fingers, and clicked it into place. A blast of floral perfume made me sneeze.

My mother stared. "What's wrong? You look a bit...shaky."

"Something weird just happened." I pointed at the gnome, who had returned to the ladder and was busily tying a vine to the trellis. "He came over and just stood there, watching me. And the next thing I knew, I was having a vision. Of him and his gnome buddies trying to escape from something chasing them. It was freaky."

My mother smiled smugly and patted my shoulder. "Now, isn't that something? He was communicating with you. Trying to tell you where they came from. They've never done that with anyone else, as far as I know. Except me, of course. You should go to the processing center or even the preserve and see if any other entities will open up to you. Madeline, I'm pleased! I always thought you might develop the gift one day."

An iron band squeezed my chest. *Please, no. Anything but that.* Taking baby steps toward becoming a bruja was one thing; developing a psychic connection with entities was another. And if it meant entities were drawn to me, it would be career-ending.

No, thank you.

My mother chatted nonstop while I drove across town, which took longer than usual because a section of Wilshire Boulevard had been closed due to entities crawling out of the ground in the park between the art museum and the tar pits. That place had always been an entity hot spot.

We had plenty of time to talk about how we were going to sneak her into Chavez Ravine.

My mother had almost prevented me from getting my job. Not that she had done anything in particular, but her affinity for entities had made her a magnet for their kind. They seemed to seek her out, which had made the board very wary of bringing me on. They had not had an entity appearance before, one of the reasons the community had become such an expensive place to live. I'd had to convince them I would never allow my mother to visit the neighborhood before they would even consider me for the position.

But, I rationalized, that had been before I concocted a protection spell to keep entities out of Chavez Ravine—with

Lencha's help—and it was before I had realized I needed my mother to help catch our killer Cucuy.

Still, if anyone saw her, I would have a difficult time explaining it.

We entered Chavez Ravine through the Bishop gate. While I chatted with the guard, my mother pretended to be looking for something in the back seat so he wouldn't see her face. Moments later, I was driving toward Phantom's Pass.

Beside me, my mother kept up a commentary. "Oh! I can't believe I'm here. It's beautiful! It's simply beautiful! Look at these houses. They're so big!"

She gushed all the way to the parking lot at the trailhead. We got out of the Jeep. She might have been dressed like Audrey Hepburn, but at least my mother had worn sensible shoes. I took her by the elbow while we made our way up to the pass.

"And you think this is where that thing is hiding out?" She seemed nervous, which surprised me. Entities didn't scare her in the least, even ghouls, so she must have been way outside her comfort zone.

"I'm almost sure of it," I replied, steering her around a cluster of boulders. "Are you sensing anything?"

My mother pulled away. "I just got here! Patience, Madeline, patience. This is like steaming tamales. It cannot be rushed."

We'd walked for about fifteen minutes when my mother abruptly stopped in a small, shaded clearing.

"What is it?" I whispered, my heart racing.

She held up a warning hand. Head cocked to one side, she appeared to be listening. Slowly, she closed her eyes.

And this was one of the big differences between me and my mother, besides her massive ego, that is: I had no patience. She could take all the time in the world, sensing and feeling. All I could feel was anxiety, knowing I was falling behind on my very long to-do list.

I was in agony, standing around, waiting for her, so I found a smooth boulder, sat down, and took out my phone to check messages. But after a few moments, I realized it was strangely quiet in the woods—no critters rustling in the brush, no birds chirping overhead.

A prickle of unease crept up my spine. I was glad I had brought my baton, slingshot, and ammo, just in case.

Something did not feel right.

I slipped a steel ball from the pouch hanging from my belt loop.

My mother's eyes snapped open.

"Something is here," she whispered. "I can feel its energy. It's strong. *Very* strong. It's hungry. Starving."

I stood up from my boulder, pulse racing. "What is it?"

"I don't know. But it's old. Ancient." She turned and began to walk back down toward the parking lot.

I trotted after her. "Is that it? You're done?"

She ignored me and picked up her pace.

"Mother," I said, grabbing her elbow. "Talk to me. Is it El Cucuy?"

She wriggled free. "I don't know. I couldn't get any images. But it doesn't want us here. We need to leave. Now."

Chapter 29

I had known my mother to be many things: self-centered, driven, critical, flamboyant, vocal, successful. But as we hurried back down the trail to the Jeep, I saw in her something I had never seen before: fear.

She had gone pale under her bronzer and kept reaching into her blouse to pull out a small pouch on a long silver chain. A protection sachet.

I didn't ask where she had gotten it, but she hadn't made it. Our family hobby, brujería, had skipped her entirely, so the sachet probably provided peace of mind—or perhaps a bit of stagecraft—but not a real defense against supernatural baddies.

When we arrived at the Jeep, the birdsong had returned, and squirrels were once again going about their business. My mother practically threw her body into the vehicle and crossed herself. She had always treated religion as an insurance policy, something one turned to in case of emergency, so whatever she had sensed in Phantom's Pass had to be serious.

"I need to lay down," she said in a shaky voice. "Please. Take me to your house."

Well, crap. My plan had been to drive my mother directly back to Beverly Hills. No pit stops, no drama. I had plenty of things to do at home, like laundry and cooking ahead for what was sure to be a busy week.

But none of those things seemed possible with my mother pacing around, sucking all the energy out of the place.

Her agitation eased when we reached La Loma and disappeared entirely as I pulled into my driveway. She was practically quivering with excitement while we made our way up the path.

"Oh, Maddy. I've seen this house in family photos so many times, but never in person! It's lovely! And the landscaping...so tasteful!"

I guided her to the small guest room, where the drama returned. She collapsed onto the bed, hands covering her eyes. I went into the kitchen and poured a glass of water. When I returned, Sam was lying next to her, his big head resting on her stomach.

"Your gatito is a sweet thing," she said, her eyes still closed.

I glared at Sam, who blinked at me innocently. My standoffish cat snuggling with my mother felt like the ultimate betrayal.

"Since when do you like cats?" I sounded like a sullen child.

Her eyes flicked open. "I don't. But he's nice. And a very handsome specimen. Is he some exotic breed?"

"He's a Bengal. He showed up one day and just moved in."

My mother pushed herself up on her elbows. Sam meowed loudly at the disruption.

"He did, did he? Well. Witches have familiars, don't they? Maybe he's yours."

I barked out a laugh. "Him? I don't think so."

Sam flicked his tail a few times. I stared at him, reconsidering. He *had* helped me before—doing battle with a hummingbird Hernan Frias had sent to spy on us, guiding me in my casting of spells. And, of course, the act of kitty karma with Bevlov's iced tea.

Was that the sort of thing a familiar did?

"Maybe he is," I conceded.

169

My mother flopped back on the bed, pulling Sam with her.

"I'll leave you two alone," I said. "Holler if you need anything."

I pulled the door shut. Suspecting she would have a nice, long nap, I threw in a load of laundry, cleaned the bathroom, and started a batch of pinto beans using a pressure cooker. Then I poked around in the freezer and pulled out a cut of pork for chili verde. Since it was too hot to turn on the oven, I set about roasting tomatillos, sliced onion, and chili in the air fryer.

After everything was blended and simmering on the stove, I checked in with Ron and Bailey. All was quiet in the command center, and Bailey seemed to be knocking it out of the park with her door-to-door security evaluations.

In the backyard, I watered my herbs and talked to them in a nice, soothing voice—something I had read about when I was in my teens but had never bothered to practice. It occurred to me it might have been why I hadn't killed them yet, like I had every other plant I had ever owned.

Back in the kitchen, I was stirring the chili verde when my mother gave a little cry from the sunroom. I assumed Sam had finally gone back to his violent ways, but I found my mother in front of the workbench, holding Little Lencha in both hands.

"Everything all right in here?" I was still clutching my wooden spoon.

My mother spun around, her eyes swamped with tears. "Is this my aunt? Is this Lencha?"

I nodded. She raised the figurine to her lips and gently kissed the top of its head.

"She's beautiful. Where did you get her?"

"My friend Julia Suarez. She's a ceramic artist. She has a shop in Palo Verde."

"Such talent! Do you think she would make one for me? Does she take commissions?"

I thought for a moment, then shrugged. "We can ask. She's driven more by inspiration than money, but we can ask."

My mother appeared a bit crestfallen. She set Little Lencha down carefully and began to inspect the rest of my workbench.

Her tears were gone, and her judgy demeanor returned.

I knew that look and braced myself for the onslaught.

"Madeline." She gestured grandly toward my bowls of dried herbs. "Why aren't these covered?" She clucked her teeth and shook her head. "They'll get dusty. And dry." She reached into a bowl, plucked something out, and held it high in the air. "Look! A cat hair. Honestly, you should know better. You need to protect the purity of your ingredients."

My skin felt like it was growing bristles. "If Sam is my familiar, I'm sure it's fine."

"This is serious," she chided. "These are the tools of your craft, hija. You need to show them respect."

Apparently, in my mother's world, being a psychic qualified one to dole out advice on magic.

She ran her hand over the old wooden workbench. "So, this is where my mother worked. I never thought I'd live to see it. Or the house. And to think it passed right by me and straight on to you." She sighed. "I would have given anything to live here, but it seems fate had other plans."

Despite myself, a lump formed in my throat. My mother had often spoken of Chavez Ravine and how her mother, Liliana Bantacorte, had fled during the evictions but never received the letter from the city inviting her to reclaim her property. If that letter had made its way to Liliana in Salinas, my mother would have inherited the house. We would have had a place to go when life with my abusive father had become unbearable. Our lives might have turned out very differently.

While I was the rightful owner of my grandmother's house, my mother deserved my compassion.

I crossed the room and wrapped her in a hug. Her body relaxed. She reached up and patted my cheek.

"Something else I never thought I'd see. Affection from my daughter." She plucked the wooden spoon from my hand. "Now, if you can please give me a tour of the rest of the house."

I had hugged the woman countless times, but I let it go. Sam followed us from room to room.

"It's so bright and cheery!" she gushed. "I love all the colors and the fabrics. I had no idea you had such design sense."

I plumped up a pillow. "I don't. This is all thanks to Julia. She took me shopping."

"Well, she certainly does have an eye." My mother sniffed the air. "It smells awfully good in here. What are you making?"

Whoops. I hadn't counted on the aroma of chili verde turning my mother's short visit into a dinner party, but that's exactly what it had done.

We made a salad and ate the chili verde and beans with a side of fresh corn tortillas. Sam sat on the windowsill and watched us.

"It's not very hygienic to let that animal up on the counters where you prepare food."

"Well, there's only so much I can do. Besides, he's constantly cleaning himself."

Sam meowed loudly.

"Yes, but he is a cat. They eat mice, don't they? And their paws are in the kitty litter." She shuddered. "Well, your house, your business." She gave a martyred sigh. "It's probably time we get going."

She didn't have to ask me twice. Within minutes, we were in the Jeep.

"Oh! I just remembered something," my mother said.

Of course she did. Would this visit never end?

"Before we leave, can you please stop at Muertos Café? I've heard so much about it, and I'd love to get some of their pan dulce."

I stared at her, aghast. "Mom, no. People will recognize you. And then the board will find out you were here, and they'll throw a fit."

"This is so annoying." She crossed her arms in front of her chest and pouted. "Fine. What if I stay in the car and you go in for me?"

"All right," I relented. After all, she had done me a favor by joining me in Phantom's Pass.

Minutes later, I drove into the back parking lot at La Loma Plaza and parked under a tree. My mother opened the passenger side window.

"I can't believe I need to stay in the car like a dog."

"Your idea, remember? I'll be quick."

I jogged across the lot and into the back door of the restaurant.

The place was packed, and I had to wait in line for what felt like forever. When I finally made it up to the front, I ordered an assortment of pan dulce and a couple of iced mochas to-go, then hustled back to the car.

Someone was talking with my mother through her open window.

My heart sank like a stone.

It was Hernan Frias wearing linen pants and a jaunty straw hat. I hurried over to do damage control. But as I drew closer, Hernan laughed while my mother gestured vigorously.

I stood frozen in place. They were so engrossed in their conversation that neither noticed me. I had assumed Hernan would be outraged to find my mother in Chavez Ravine, but he appeared to be downright charmed.

While I watched in disbelief, I realized they weren't just having a little chat. They were *flirting*.

My mother giggled. Hernan chuckled. I gagged.

Taking a deep, calming breath, I strode toward the Jeep.

My mother spotted me first. "Oh, look who's coming by to do a welfare check."

Hernan took off his hat and gave a little bow. "I thought, who could possibly have left this poor woman alone in a car in this heat!" His eyes narrowed slightly. "And now I know."

"It looks like she survived." My voice sounded as if sandpaper could talk.

"I was telling Professor Frias about what we were doing in Phantom's Pass."

My mother couldn't seem to stop smiling. I desperately wished she would. It was just gross.

Hernan's chest puffed out. "I told her she was brave to go in there. And it was fascinating to hear your mother explain her process. She's a very accomplished woman."

I could hardly believe my ears. Since we had first met, Hernan had repeatedly bashed my mother, but there he was, falling all over himself. I wasn't sure how much more I could take.

Hernan dragged his gaze away from her and turned to me. "It was a little risky, you bringing her in here. I understand the necessity, and I think we can all agree to keep this to ourselves, no?"

I nodded. "Of course. Any luck researching the Cucuy?"

"Unfortunately, no. The books I have made no mention of any weaknesses, and my friend in Mexico knew of nothing either.

I was going to call you when I got home after a bite of lunch at Muertos Café." He glanced at my mother. "It is too bad you can't join me."

My mother simpered. "She won't let me."

I pushed past Hernan and handed my mother her mocha through the open window. "Enjoy your lunch," I said over my shoulder.

Hernan ignored me. "Goodbye, Malena! It was lovely meeting you in person! I do hope I run into you again soon!"

When we drove off, I peered into the rearview mirror. Hernan was still standing there, waving, hat in hand, looking flushed.

Apparently, my mother could charm scary entities *and* pompous old brujos alike.

Chapter 30

While my coffee maker rumbled away on the countertop, I opened a can of cat food and scooped some into Sam's bowl. When the carafe was just about full, I filled my mug and took it into the sunroom to catch up on messages from my cozy couch.

The doorbell rang.

Someone was about to get an eyeful of makeup-free Maddy.

I put my mug down and answered the door. It was a delivery driver with a huge floral arrangement from Stu. The note inside read: "Clare told me what happened. You deserve this and more. Can't wait to see you."

As soon as I had finished tapping out a message of thanks to Stu, the doorbell rang again.

I opened the front door and picked up a small cardboard box from the porch. After taking it into the kitchen, I sliced through the packing tape and lifted the lid. A skeletal figure wearing a hooded gold cape stared back at me. It was a beautiful deck of Santa Muerte tarot cards nestled in purple tissue paper.

There was a gift receipt inside. My mother had sent it. While I pondered this strange gift, my phone rang, and I saw her name on the screen.

"Did you get them?" she asked without preamble.

"Yes. But I'd love to know *why* you sent them."

My mother sniffed. "It was Hernan's idea, actually. He thought the cards might help you find out if El Cucuy is your killer."

There was only one problem with that. "Mom, I don't know anything about Santa Muerte. I can't just hit her up with a favor out of the blue."

"She'll understand. This is a desperate situation."

"Mother. She's Our Lady of the Holy Death. Saint Death. As in, the personification of death itself."

"See? You know more than you're letting on. You'll be fine. If you have any questions, Hernan said you are welcome to call him."

I barked out a laugh. "He did, did he?"

"Yes, he did. And by the way, he is absolutely *nothing* like you described him. I was expecting some sort of charlatan, the way you went on about the poor man."

I bit my tongue. That is exactly how *he* had described *her*.

It was no use arguing.

"There is another problem," I said. "I know nothing about tarot cards, so I can't imagine I'm going to have much luck with them."

"Then it's too bad you haven't taken your craft more seriously," my mother replied sharply. "You owe the people you are supposed to protect your best effort, Madeline, and if that means asking Hernan for help, then quit making excuses and get to it."

And with that, she hung up.

The skeletal face of Santa Muerte stared at me from the cardboard box. Her expression was skeptical with a hint of disapproval. So was mine.

And yet, I called Hernan. We decided to meet in the historical records room at the library in Palo Verde Plaza.

An hour and a half later, I found him sitting alone at a table, surrounded by old black and white photos.

"Hello, Maddy. Your mother says you got her little gift this morning."

They'd been messaging each other already?

"I did. How did you know?"

"We exchanged numbers yesterday."

He gestured at the pile of pictures. I sat down and picked one up.

It showed a short, crooked street with small clapboard houses nestled against a tree-lined hill. No sidewalks. Just a rutted dirt road and a few men working on an old car. Chavez Ravine had come a long, long way since those days. The community was barely recognizable, except for the hills. There were plenty of those.

"You know, Maddy, if you ever have some spare time, I can use a hand digitizing these."

"That's something I don't have a lot of these days. Have you thought of putting out a call for volunteers?"

Hernan frowned. "I'm not sure I would be willing to trust just anyone with these photos. They're our history. You know, there are some people who deny it ever happened. Eviction deniers. They'd love to get their hands on these and destroy the evidence."

Hernan had always been a zealous protector of Chavez Ravine, but he now sounded downright paranoid.

"Your mother says you're worried about connecting with Santa Muerte. That you somehow got the idea she's—I don't know—scary?" He lifted his eyebrows.

I nodded. "Well, she *is* a death figure, and she looks like the grim reaper. So yeah, I take that seriously. Before I do anything with those cards, I want to make sure I know what I'm getting myself into."

"Then let me explain her history," he said. "It's fascinating."

178

Professor Frias launched into a lecture. He started with Aztec deities, the representation of bodies with the flesh removed, then moved on to the Spanish conquest. And, because he couldn't help himself, Hernan went on and on about the theories involving her origins, the ideas she symbolized, and how she had come to be revered by the working-class people in poverty-stricken parts of Mexico.

All of that was interesting but not helpful. I still had no idea what to do with the deck of cards, though understanding Santa Muerte's origin did make her less intimidating.

Hernan kept going, explaining how gangsters had adopted the folk saint, which infuriated him.

"When the cops found some drug lords had shrines to her, the press went crazy. All that coverage tainted her reputation. It wasn't fair. She was venerated by people from all walks of life because she was without judgment."

"Are you a devotee?" I asked, keeping my voice light.

Hernan shook his head. "No. But that doesn't mean I don't understand her appeal."

It was time to get things back on track. "And why do you think she would be helpful to me? Can she help me track down El Cucuy?"

"Now, that's an interesting question." Hernan leaned back in his chair and formed a steeple with his hands. "It all depends on you. She's very powerful, and she doesn't mess around. She gets things done—and fast. But you have to persuade her to help you."

Cold fingers raked my spine. "How am I supposed to do that?"

Hernan reached across the table, grabbed my hands, and gave them a little shake. His skin was dry and warm but not unpleasant. "With respect."

179

"Hernan, I'm looking for some help here. My mother seems to think you can give me some hints about how to use the cards to figure out if our bad guy is El Cucuy. Is that the case, or isn't it?

Hernan let go of my hands and sat back in his chair.

"Maddy, I don't think you understand the gift that Lencha gave you. You have tremendous power, but you must learn how to put it to work. Everything else—your herbs, the chilis in your garden, the cards—those are just tools. They are useless until they're handled by someone with skill and knowledge. You have everything you need, but you need to find a way to channel your power.

"That's the only way those Santa Muerte cards will be able to help you. And Maddy, I know you can do it. I can see you have everything you need to solve these murders and much, much more. Your mother sees it too. We can encourage you, but that's all. The rest is up to you."

A lump rose in my throat. Hernan, the man who had opposed me at every turn and caused me endless aggravation, had just delivered a pep talk.

Before I got all misty-eyed and embarrassed myself, I jumped to my feet with a husky, "Thank you," and hurried out of the room.

Chapter 31

The moment I walked in the door, I cranked up the air conditioning and made a pot of yerba buena tea. After my bizarre meeting with Hernan Frias, I needed something to settle my nervous stomach.

While the water was heating up, I lit some vanilla-scented candles in the living room.

And for the third time that day, the doorbell rang. "Now what?"

I yanked open the front door in time to watch a delivery man jog toward his truck at the curb.

"I left it behind the chair," he called.

I retrieved a small box and brought it inside. It required scissors and patience, but I was finally able to cut through the layers of brown paper and bubble wrap. Inside was a figurine of Santa Muerte, her long hooded cloak painted red and gold, a scythe in one hand and a red rose in the other. It was beautiful but foreboding.

While I admired the figurine, dark eyes stared back at me.

A note read: "This should help with visualization."

Another gift from my mother.

I appreciated the thought, but figurines and cards weren't going to catch El Cucuy.

"It's just you and me, then," I said, carrying the little statue into the living room.

After setting her down on the coffee table, I sat cross-legged on the floor, opened the deck of cards, and shuffled them. I put the deck on the table next to the figurine, closed my eyes, and tried to feel the power Hernan had said I had inside me.

I recalled his words and the confidence he had felt that I could find the murderer, whatever it was…that my mother felt the same way.

While I couldn't say I felt powerful, I was relaxed. My breathing had settled into a slow, deep rhythm, and the only sound I heard was the steady beating of my heart. After a few moments, I opened my eyes and stared at Santa Muerte.

"We hardly know each other, and it seems a bit rude to just start asking you for things, but something evil has moved into our community, and people are afraid. With respect, I'm asking you to help me figure out who or what it is so I can deal with it. Please."

I reached up, drew the first card, and turned it over.

El Diablo. The Devil. An interesting way to start.

The next card was La Muerte. There had been three deaths in Chavez Ravine, so that made sense.

I understood the meanings behind the cards. *That* was new.

The Tower followed—a symbol of upheaval. There had been plenty of chaos in Chavez Ravine. We were on a roll. My fingers suddenly felt warm and began to glow red, a sign my magic was activating.

The Moon and the Hanged Man. La Luna was linked with illusions and secrets. El Colgado, the Hanged Man, was more perplexing. It usually symbolized a situation requiring a new perspective. Perhaps that made sense, but what kind of perspective?

I decided the next card would be the last.

It was The Hermit. The brightly colored skeletal man with luxurious dark hair looked an awful lot like Hernan Frias. Also similar to Hernan, The Hermit studied the mysteries of life. But I wasn't sure quite what to make of that card.

I wished I had drawn the card for strength—the man wearing a Luche Libre mask, stomping on a dragon. But no.

I stacked the six cards next to the Santa Muerte figurine and tapped them with an index finger glowing the color of a Cascabel chili.

Nothing happened.

I needed to calm my mind, to focus.

Even though I closed my eyes and took a few deep breaths, my thoughts skittered away in all directions. I needed to keep my question front and center.

Is it El Cucuy? Is it El Cucuy? Is it El Cucuy?

It became a chant in my head.

I sensed a movement behind my shoulder, then the bump of a nose against the back of my head. It was Sam, purring loudly. A moment later, a gentle weight rested on my shoulder—Sam's paw—his touch warm and reassuring.

Calm washed over me, as if that paw was grounding me in the moment. I closed my eyes and reached behind to scratch his head. He purred so loudly it sent a vibration through my body.

I focused on the question.

Is it El Cucuy?

When I finally opened my eyes, the cards were in a new configuration. They formed a circle around the little figurine.

Had I done that? With her help? Or was she trying to send me a message?

I stared at the cards, each holding a piece of the puzzle I was desperately trying to solve. But no answer to my question materialized.

My eyes drifted up to the Santa Muerte statue. It suddenly seemed alert, watching me with an intensity that sent shivers down my spine. I wasn't afraid. In fact, I was *excited*, like I was on the edge of something.

Taking another deep breath, I closed my eyes and allowed my mind to drift. I needed to trust the process, and myself.

It was like I was dreaming, but I wasn't asleep. Images flashed behind my eyelids.

Rolling hills at night. A full moon. I recognized the area. It was Chavez Ravine but long ago, before all the big houses, paved streets, and landscaped plazas. Something was emerging from a cave. A crooked, hooded figure, its shape all wrong, with a ghoulish white face and long arms covered in black, bristly hair.

It was El Cucuy. There was no doubt. He sniffed the air, the ragged mouth snarling. And he loped down the hill toward the lights of the houses below, but I couldn't follow him. Nor could I stop him.

And then came the shrieks of a terrified child. Moments later, a man and a woman began screaming. El Cucuy came back up the hill, the child clutched to its chest. They disappeared inside the cave.

I covered my ears so I wouldn't have to listen to what came afterward.

More unwanted images flashed before me, each one more horrifying than the last. A sharp, gnawing sensation in my stomach made me double over. I was feeling the hunger of El Cucuy, starving for the flesh of human children. And then time was speeding by, and the hunger was replaced by a new equally terrible feeling.

Loneliness.

A monster all alone in the world, without a mate, without companionship. An outcast living on the fringes of a happy little community he would never be free to join. Banished to a nowhere land until he was called back by a frustrated mother who had invoked his name.

El Cucuy sat on a rock, staring up at the moon, radiating sadness and isolation. He was tired of his life and wanted, more than anything, to become human.

I felt myself being drawn to the monster, ever closer, until I could hear his thoughts and see through his eyes.

He made a pact with a mysterious and powerful being. El Cucuy swore to stop taking children in exchange for his humanity. I sensed his relief while he began to shed his monstrous appearance, but I also felt his hunger. He was starving, still craving the lives he had sworn to give up.

My eyes snapped open, my throat dry, blood roaring in my ears.

Sam had moved and was now sitting next to me on the floor, his green eyes staring at Santa Muerte. Her bony face appeared pleased, even smug.

But I wasn't so happy. I still had questions.

It was time to talk to my team. I called a meeting and headed to the command center.

Chapter 32

"Sorry about the short notice, but I've been doing some research this morning. I want to share what I've learned with you because, frankly, I've answered some questions and come up with new ones."

"No problem, boss." Ron was obviously happy for any diversion from his heatmap-monitoring job.

Bailey nodded. "Same here. I'm about done with my home visits, so I'm ready for something new."

I loved her attitude, but I just hoped she still felt that way once she heard what I had to say.

"Okay. Well, as you know, these killings have been very unusual. The evidence has been inconclusive. Unusual wounds, foul odors, and second-story windows in two of the cases support conflicting theories. Now, it's not a competition to see who can solve the killings first, but I believe we've had one big advantage over the LAPD: we've been open to the possibility the killer is an entity or some kind of non-human creature.

"That's why we thought Dog Face Bride might be a suspect, though we've since ruled her out. And we've all known the pale man in a hoodie might be our culprit. He's been seen in the gully and was caught on film near Phantom's Pass, but we don't know much more about him than that."

I cleared my throat and took a sip of water for the next part.

"I'm going to shift gears, so stay with me. Many of the entities that have infiltrated Los Angeles since the earthquake swarm have roots in mythology or folk culture. Chaneques and

Chupacabras come from Mexican folklore, gnomes come from European traditions, etcetera. If we look to folklore for possible suspects, particularly ones that have been seen in Chavez Ravine in the past, we have one likely suspect: El Cucuy, the child-snatching monster from Latin American lore. I've been doing some research on the Cucuy, and I'd like to talk about what I've discovered."

Justin groaned, hands covering his eyes. "My mom scared the crap out of me with stories of the Cucuy. Please tell me you're not about to say he's real."

Ron laughed grimly. "Buckle up, butter cup."

Before Ron could hijack my meeting, I continued.

"First, I'll start with the answers. I believe the Cucuy is living in or near Phantom's Pass, and I am fairly certain he's trying to become human. That means the figure I saw in the gully *was* the Cucuy, and he was headed back to his hiding spot after killing Misty Denner. It makes sense that the man in the trees in the film footage was the Cucuy, and so was the man the gardener saw up at Bishop Circles. Same clothing, same pale face. Plus, nothing else explains that awful smell at the crime scenes.

"But—and here's where the new questions come in—I am also certain El Cucuy has had to change his ways. He can't take children and eat them anymore. This doesn't mean—"

"Hold on. Why can't he take kids any longer?" Justin was a young father obviously looking for some good news to bring home to his worried wife.

"It's complicated, but in order to become human, he's made a pact of some sort. He can't keep taking children, or he'll revert to his old self."

"So, that means he's harmless," Ron said. "The Cucuy is back, but he's just a regular guy. So, we still have no idea who our murderer is."

"I don't know about that." Justin's voice rose. "If he's hanging out in Phantom's Pass, that would explain why he's attacking members of the film crew. They're making the movie right in his backyard."

Bailey had been staring into space, but Justin's words snapped her out of her trance. "Wait a minute. He can't take children, right? But all our victims have been short. Both the women were petite, and Brad Plante, the guy in Bishop Circles, wasn't much over five feet. So, in the Cucuy's eyes, maybe small adults are the next best thing to children."

And with those words, everything fell into place. *Click, click, click.*

I nearly ran over and gave Bailey a big kiss.

My euphoria lasted a whole minute. Since we were certain the Cucuy was our perp, as Ron would say, we had to come up with a way to take him out.

I left the office a little early and went home. Though I was still on the clock, what I had to do was best done in the privacy of my own living room.

When I arrived home, I opened the French doors so Sam could run out and do his business, sorted through the mail, and poured a glass of iced tea. After putting the tea on an end table, I plopped down on the couch, unsure of how to go about my next task.

Could I manage another vision but, this time, one that showed me how to slay the Cucuy? Or conjure a spell to turn a slingshot or baton into Cucuy-killers? I really had no idea what I was asking for, except for an end to the Cucuy.

I stared at the Santa Muerte figurine. She was right where I had left her, surrounded by the tarot cards I had drawn earlier. A ray of late afternoon sunlight fell across the ring of tarot. But my perfect circle of cards was off. I had arranged six of them around the saint of death—three on one side and three on the other. But now there was a seventh card throwing off the symmetry.

I picked it up and turned it over. The Five of Swords. The colorful illustration summed up my situation. A skeletal woman wearing a wide-brimmed hat was trapped in a maze, with five swords pointing at her head.

Unlike the last time I had used the tarot cards, I wasn't getting a reading on The Five of Swords. I had no idea what it meant.

With both the cat and Santa Muerte watching, I called my mother.

"How did it go?" Her tone was light, as if I had gone shopping for a dress.

"Better than I hoped," I said. "It's a long story, but I was able to confirm that the Cucuy is our murderer. It took six cards and some concentration, but that mystery is solved. However, the Five of Swords just popped up, and I don't know what that means."

"Well, that card is very *you*, with all your inner conflict. The swords symbolize the things that drag you down instead of pushing you to reach your full potential. Nothing you can't fix by putting a little more effort into your craft instead of expecting your great-aunt to bail you out."

"Mother, please. Back to the Five of Swords."

My mother covered the phone and shouted something. "Sorry. Some new gnomes popped up, and I haven't had a moment's peace all day." She cleared her throat. "It sounds like you're going to need to muster all your strength and courage to fight El Cucuy."

No shit. "That's a little vague, Mom. Like, how?"

"Madre mia de Dios, you're the fighter, not me. How am I supposed to know?"

Is my mother being intentionally unhelpful? "Is there anything in that card that suggests how I might go about it?"

She scoffed. "I'm not there, am I? I couldn't possibly tell you."

"You're a psychic!"

"And you're magic, or so you say, so *you* figure it out. Look, Maddy. That card was meant for *you*. You need to open yourself up to its meaning. Have you tried that yet, or did you call hoping Mommy would do your homework for you again?" She laughed, a hint of bitterness in her voice.

And with that, she hung up.

I screamed into a pillow. Which, strangely, calmed me down.

I picked up the Five of Swords again and studied it. The skeletal figure might have been trapped in a maze, but she wore a determined expression, one bony fist raised in the air at the swords. And those weapons, they seemed to radiate with a silver glow all their own.

My eyes blurred. I blinked to clear them, and the skeleton's hand shot out, grabbed a sword, and brandished it. The sword glowed and shimmered.

Startled, I dropped the card. It fluttered to the floor.

The tarot card had literally told me to get a magical, glowing sword. Is that how it worked? No complicated riddle to solve, no reading between the lines, even. Just "Hey, grab a sword and stab the damn thing."

Maybe that was my answer. I needed a sword to slay El Cucuy. Not just any sword, but one with some magical *oomph*. Why did it have to be any more complicated than that?

I stood up and, not knowing what else to do, curtsied to Santa Muerte.

"Thank you," I said stiffly. "Thank you for all of your help today."

Chapter 33

Not many people would know how to go about buying a sword, but I did. Thanks to Julia, I had been to the NoHo Axe Throwing Bar, and if anyone could introduce me to a sword seller, it was the guys who hung out there. That meant driving to North Hollywood.

I hopped in the Jeep, and as soon as I hit the Five Freeway, I called Jo at the Occult Affairs Command Center for a catch-up.

"I haven't heard from you in forever," she grumbled.

"It's been kind of busy up here."

She chuckled. "How are things going with Leesa Bevlov?"

"How do you think? She's always icing me out or actively throwing me under the bus. Neither is very nice, but I can deal." I paused long enough to honk at a driver who had swerved in front of me. "You hearing anything about her investigation?"

Jo cleared her throat. "As a matter of fact, I am." She lowered her voice. "But you need to keep it to yourself. Bevlov's over at Western Studios, grilling everyone who worked on the *Phantom's Pass* movie. The word is, she thinks someone there had it out for the three victims."

I guessed she was right, in a way. El Cucuy hung out near the film studio.

"Is she getting anywhere?"

"Well, she's pissing a lot of people off. You know how she is. Steve Zhao swung by to see me, by the way. He says you've been supportive. Which I appreciate because I know how you feel about nerds invading your territory."

My hands spasmed on the steering wheel. Steve wasn't just invading *my* territory. He and his nerd buddies were probably tromping through El Cucuy's backyard. *Shit.* The guy deserved a warning. I was anxious to get off the phone and see if he was all right.

"He's a good guy," I said, distracted by a sea of red lights ahead.

I fought my way to the first exit ramp to avoid whatever the mess was, which meant a detour through Griffith Park and the zoo. As I was passing the zoo's parking lot, children and adults were running in all directions.

"Hey, Jo. Are you looking at the heatmap?"

I knew she was by the string of curses she unleashed. "This is *not* what I need right now."

As if there was ever a good time for an entity emergence. I slowed down for a better look.

"It's a big one."

"Not a troll!" Jo nearly shouted.

I slammed on the brakes and hopped out of the Jeep. "No. It looks like a giant worm in the middle of the soccer field. It's got horns. Tail is still in the ground. It's swaying back and forth. It's either stuck or it's really confused. Want me to babysit this for you until you can get someone here?"

"I don't know when that's going to be. We're short-staffed, and I have everyone at Exposition Park. We've got a Banshee outbreak in the middle of a school tour, and it's nuts."

The upper half of the horned worm was flopping around, trying to wriggle out of the hole. A group of parents holding little kids under their arms stampeded past me. I sighed. My Occult Affairs days were behind me, but Jo was my friend, and she needed a favor. She had done plenty for me in the past.

"I've got some Smoke Bombs," I said. "I'll take care of it until you can get a cleanup crew here."

I pulled off the road and took a box of pouches from the back, then made my way across the grassy field under a blazing sun. By the time I reached the worm—which was much larger and nastier-looking up close—my back was slick with sweat.

I kept a safe distance while I studied my quarry.

The worm let out a deep, guttural growl when I approached, its eyes glowing a milky white. With any luck, it was blind. I inched closer and got my answer.

Its mouth opened, revealing a hodgepodge of nubby gray teeth and a few in front shaped like daggers. A long, forked tongue the color of bologna shot out of its mouth, and I had to jump back to avoid it.

A few people shouted warnings at me, but I waved them off.

I had forgotten just how unpleasant some entities could be. Though, I preferred dealing with that worm than with El Cucuy.

It was time to put the thing out of his misery.

The worm's eyes shifted color—from white, to green, to yellow. That was interesting. I had never seen an entity do that before. But I had never come across a giant horned worm with scales. I wondered if it was a dragon. It didn't appear to have wings, but they might have still been down in the hole, with the rest of it.

I didn't think it was a dragon, but I wanted to knock it out before the rest of it emerged and proved me wrong.

The worm let out a long and miserable-sounding roar. Its eyes had gone blood red, which made it look even more disgusting.

I took a Smoke Bomb from the box, feeling the familiar weight of the sedative powder in my hand. When I tossed it toward the creature, it let out a piercing screech, making my ears ring. The smoke cast an eerie purple haze over the area. The worm thrashed around wildly, its tongue trying to reach me.

Through the fog, the worm's eyes cycled through colors like a disco ball. Mesmerized, I found myself drawn closer to it despite the danger of its teeth and tongue.

A dizzying wave washed over me. My head spun. It felt as though the ground beneath my feet had abruptly tilted, leaving me off-balance. Another earthquake?

Please, no. Not now.

A flash of light made me throw up my hands, but the glare was behind my eyes. When the light faded, I pictured a vast underground cavern, crystals clinging to the walls, the air heavy with moisture. The sound of dripping water echoed through the chamber. And then a desolate countryside pockmarked with fiery pits, towering mountains rising in the distance.

The worm moved quickly while an enormous shadow crossed over the land. I sensed the worm's terror and then relief when it burrowed into a cavern, pushing its way in, only to find itself in a strange and sunny land.

I stumbled back, overwhelmed by the intensity of the image.

That was the second time an entity had taken over my mind and, like the vision I'd had with the gnome at my mother's place, the second time I had seen a shadow chasing entities into the ground.

The worm let out another mournful, pleading roar. I could wonder about the weird mind meld later.

After throwing a Smoke Bomb on the ground, I gave it a good stomp. The purple stuff covered the top of my foot and rose into the air.

The worm wobbled, then flopped to the side.

I heaved a sigh of relief. Big as he was, it only took two pouches to knock him out. I felt tired, all the way to my bones, and leaned forward, hands on my knees. A woman rushed over and offered me a bottle of cold water.

"Thank you," I murmured, then sank down next to the worm.

It wasn't just a mindless beast. Something evil had hunted it, and in its desperate attempt to escape, it had ended up here, in a world where it didn't belong.

I reached out and touched the worm's scaly hide. "You poor sucker."

Two Occult Affairs officers came running up. I recognized one of them. It was Malik, the former barista at Muertos Café and Bailey Nixon's somewhat new boyfriend.

They skidded to a stop a few yards from where I was sitting next to the worm.

Malik had cut his hair, but a lock still flopped over one eye, just like it had when he served up delicious cafecitos. "Whoa. The Dump will need to send over a truck to haul this thing away. It's way too big for our crates."

The Dump was the not-so-nice nickname for the processing facility for newly emerged entities. In reality, it was quite nice, carefully designed to be as welcoming and calming as such a place could be. But Occult Affairs officers were a jaded bunch.

The other officer, a woman with a turned-up nose who appeared to be barely out of the academy, glanced down at me and smiled. "Hey, you're the famous Maddy Madrigal." She shifted her attention to the worm and frowned. "What is that thing?"

"No idea. Never seen one before." I tried to stand, but my legs felt like jelly.

Malik stuck out a hand and helped me to my feet.

I pointed at the pouch on his belt. "If this thing comes to before the truck gets here, one more of those should do the trick."

The officers began to secure the area. But I couldn't shake the image of the giant shadow chasing the worm. I was pretty sure it was the same thing I had seen pursuing the gnomes when I had been in my mother's driveway.

What were these visions? Why were they happening now? I had worked for Occult Affairs for years, and the only thing I had ever seen were stars when I got knocked on my ass by a rogue entity.

I feared I had inherited more from my mother than good hair and skills in the kitchen.

Chapter 34

Even though it was the middle of the afternoon, the NoHo Axe Bar was busy. A raucous group of women around my age filled one lane, with a laminated photo of a handsome silver-haired man attached to the bullseye. A woman with bouncy brown hair and a spray tan aimed an axe at the photo while several friends cheered her on.

"Fuck you, Jerry!" the woman shouted, throwing the axe hard.

If Jerry had been a real person, he would have had an axe buried in his forehead.

"Nice throw," I said when I walked by.

The woman spun around. "Thanks. It's all about the motivation. Wanna join us? It's a break-up party. As in, that fucking fucker left me for some tart half his age." She was slurring her words.

"I'd love to, but I can't stay long."

In the last lane, I found Chad and Tanner, the owners of The Slingshot Academy who had trained my team, giving a lesson to a group of burly men. Both instructors wore camouflage baseball caps. Chad spotted me and hurried over. Tanner frowned, obviously annoyed his partner had left him alone to deal with their clients.

"Did we miss a message from you?" Chad asked. A nice way of asking "What are you doing here?"

"Nope. Surprise visit. I hate to interrupt, but I need a quick emergency consultation. It should only take a few minutes, and

I'd be happy to pay you for an individual lesson." Not me, personally, but from my HOA security budget.

"Not a problem," Chad said, then shouted, "I'll be right back," to Tanner, who flipped him off. "Don't let him bother you," Chad said, guiding me toward the lounge. "He's just jealous I get to spend time alone with our favorite client."

Chad couldn't help himself. He wasn't able to stop flirting, but at least he wasn't as gross about it as he used to be.

We had settled into leather easy chairs under the watchful gaze of a stuffed bison head. A server came over, and we placed our orders—iced tea for me and brew on tap for Chad.

He leaned forward, arms resting on his knees. "I am honored that you've come to me with whatever help you need." He paused, voice lowering. "Seriously. And touched."

Chad wasn't exactly handsome, but he would have had more luck with women if he didn't try so hard. I sighed.

"We have a problem up at Chavez Ravine. Something new. I can't give you the details, but I need to get a hold of some swords. Real ones, if you get my drift. Not the soft-tipped kind they use in competitions."

Chad straightened. His eyes went wide. "Wow. Yeah. Okay. I know a thing or two or three about swords. If you really want lethal force, you need a battling blade. There used to be a specialty store downtown that sold antique swords, but the guy retired. Sometimes, vendors at conventions or Renaissance fairs sell that sort of thing, but it sounds like you're on a deadline. I don't recommend buying them online. There's no way to tell what you're getting."

The server returned with our drinks. Chad gulped down his beer.

"There's an old guy who has a pretty amazing private collection of Toledo Swords. As in Toledo, Spain." Chad was

199

practically vibrating with excitement. "I don't know exactly what you're up against, but those are fucking amazing. They've got an iron core with layers of steel over it. They're flexible and durable as hell. And he claims he can trace some of them all the way back to the Conquistadores."

I knew nothing about swords, but they sounded perfect. "Do you think this old fellow would be willing to sell some of his collection?" Even if he did, I wasn't sure my budget would go that far.

Chad shrugged. "You'd have to ask him. If not, he might loan them to you. Assuming that would work for you. But he's got a big collection. And he lives pretty close to here. Just tell him I sent you his way and he'll take care of you." Chad pulled his phone from a pocket. "Here. Let me send you his contact info."

My phone chimed a moment later. When I tapped on the message from Chad, my heart skipped a beat.

The renowned collector of Toledo Swords dating back to the Conquistadores was none other than Hernan Frias.

Marta, Hernan's caretaker-turned-permanent-live-in-aide, greeted me at the door. "He's been in a much better mood since he started driving again," she said in a low voice. "But I worry about the pedestrians."

I stepped into the gloomy house, wondering how she could stand it. Though I had been inside for less than a minute, I already wanted to rip open the drapes.

"I'm glad he's finally feeling happier. I'm sure he's been hard to deal with."

She gave me a sly smile. "It's not just because he's driving again. He's met someone. I think he has a crush. He's been humming."

Oh, no. "A crush?" I said lightly. "Know anything about her?"

"Si. At least he's got taste. She's very beautiful. And muy famosa. It's Malena Bantacorte!"

Of course it was.

Marta continued. "He asked me to find her old TV shows, and we've been watching them together. She's almost as good as Walter Mercado!"

Hardly. The late astrologer had been a cultural icon of Latin America, and he was in a class of his own. My mother was undeniably charismatic, but she lacked his gift for flamboyance.

I sighed. Marta would find out eventually. "Malena Bantacorte is my mother."

"No me digas!" Marta cried.

"It's true. I'm surprised Hernan didn't mention it."

Marta eyed me up and down. "I'm not all that surprised. He's a funny one sometimes. Now that you mention it, I can see the resemblance. Although, honestly, I think you're prettier."

I actually blushed. My mother was the beauty in the family, not me. Marta just liked me because I sometimes brought treats from Muertos Café.

"Thank you," I said briskly. "Is Señor Frias around?"

"He's been in with his dusty books all morning." Marta shrugged. "It's fine by me. He's out of my hair that way."

I removed my shoes in the entryway. "Do you happen to know if he has a collection of swords?"

Marta shuddered. "Ai, yes, he does. He's got a whole room full of them, and I have to dust and polish those darn things."

Marta had a hard job. Several of them.

A few minutes later, a mystified Hernan was leading me down a dim hallway and into a dark room. When he flicked on the lights, I blinked at all the glittering steel. Swords of all shapes and sizes adorned the walls.

Hernan gestured for me to take a seat on a plush red velvet loveseat. "I don't remember telling you I collected swords."

"You didn't." I folded my hands on my lap. "Chad did. He runs the Slingshot Academy. I asked him for some recommendations, and he suggested you."

Hernan nodded. He was wearing loose, faded jeans and a Tito Puente T-shirt. This was a much more casual version of Hernan than I usually encountered. He seemed younger and more energetic too.

"I've been collecting these for many, many years. Most of them are Toledo Swords, but I have some Spanish-made falchions and rapiers too." He frowned. "Why the sudden interest in swords?"

"It's a long story, but I'm pretty sure your favorite saint told me to get my act together and kill El Cucuy with a sword."

Hernan leaned against a heavy wooden desk. "Really? Santa Muerte told you to use my swords?"

Oh, so tempting. *Why, yes, she did, and if you refuse, she'll haunt your dreams.*

But I owed the man the truth. "She didn't actually *speak* the words," I admitted. "But yeah, the cards told me to use swords. My mother sent me a statuette of Santa Muerte, and I think that supercharged things."

Hernan raked a hand through his thatch of dark hair. "If Lencha Bantacorte could hear you talk. Supercharged! I've never heard of anything so ridiculous. But if she gave you those orders, then who am I to stand in your way? El Cucuy must be killed. And if one of my swords can do it, then be my guest." His eyebrows lowered. "Do you even know how to use one?"

I took a deep breath and met Hernan's steely gaze. "I've had training in self-defense, and I can use a baton, but I wouldn't call myself an expert with a sword.

A slow and slightly alarming smile spread across his craggy face. "Well, it's a good thing you came to me then because I can show you a thing or two about wielding a sword."

He walked over to the wall lined with weapons and plucked one from the rack. It had an ornate hilt with intricate engravings.

"Most of these I bought on my trips to Spain, but this one saw some fierce battles against the Aztec Empire. I found it at a market stall in Mexico. The vendor had no idea it was the real thing."

It was my turn to frown. "Doesn't it belong in a museum?"

Hernan pointed the sword at me. "They've got storage rooms full of antiquities from the Spanish conquest. The last thing they need is more swords." He cleared his throat. "I think it's only right these get put to good use instead of being used against native people."

"How do you know they're authentic? It's not like they came with little certificates attached to them, did they?"

Hernan gave a dismissive sniff. "I know because I used my tarot cards to help me envision their history."

That got my attention. "Did Santa Muerte help you too?"

"Perhaps." Hernan might not have been a devotee of Our Lady of Holy Death, but he wasn't above appealing to her for assistance. "Don't just sit there. Come over here so I can show you what to do."

Hernan handed me the sword. It was heavier than I had expected, as hefty as a bag of sugar, but the weight was better distributed.

He quickly stepped away from me and pressed his back against the wall. "Do you feel the balance? It's nice, no?"

I nodded. It was. I gave an experimental swing. That was nice too.

"This is not an action movie," Hernan said. "Don't be in such a rush. Get the feel of it in your hand."

I rolled my eyes. "I'm not going to kill anything by standing around and showing it off."

"Always in a rush. Always trying to take shortcuts. Sword fighting is like brujería, Madeline. You need to take time to learn how to do it properly."

"Look, I'm not trying to become a master swordfighter," I snapped. "The Cucuy is out there now, maybe even stalking his next victim. I just need the basics, all right? And besides, I'm not doing this alone. I'll have my team. We just have to learn enough so we don't hurt ourselves."

Hernan stared at me, at a rare loss for words.

"Hernan, I'm just saying we need to strike a balance. We have an urgent problem, and we urgently need a solution. I don't need to become a master; I just need to be adequate. Good enough to take out the Cucuy."

"Okay. How many swords do you need?"

"One for me and four for my team."

"So, I'm going to show you, and you're going to show them?" Hernan sounded skeptical.

"That's the idea."

He studied me for a long moment. "All right. Let's get started so you can get going." He crossed the room and began rummaging around in a closet. Hernan pulled out a large plastic bin and began piling scabbards and sheaths onto the desk. "Do you want to call one of your guys to come help you with this?"

I did a quick mental calculation. The swords couldn't have weighed more than twenty-five pounds. *Easy peasy.*

Hernan went to a display on a wall and made some *mmm* sounds. After what seemed like forever, he gently lifted a slender blade from its hooks.

"This is a traditional Spanish rapier. It's lightweight and made for thrusting. In your hands, with the help of a magical boost, it should work against El Cucuy."

I took the rapier from him. It was several pounds lighter than the sword and felt very natural in my hand.

Hernan watched me closely and nodded. "Looks like a good fit. Now, let's start with the basic stance."

An hour later, I was driving home, plotting my next session with Santa Muerte. I had just reached Palo Verde when my phone rang.

"Boss." It was Ron, his voice high. "There's been an attack in Phantom's Pass. It sounds like the Cucuy."

Oh, no. Between the worm at the zoo and securing the swords for my team, I had forgotten to warn Steve Zhao about the Cucuy.

Chapter 35

I found Steve Zhao and another Occult Affairs researcher sitting on plastic chairs in the hospital waiting room.

"How's she doing? What happened?"

"She's not too bad, considering." Steve jerked his head at his companion. "This is Mark Lebowski. This is Maddy Madrigal, the head of security I was telling you about."

The entity researcher's hair was a salt-and-pepper mix, more salt than pepper, with wiry strands sticking out in all directions.

"Nice to meet you." He sounded distracted. His eyes had a faraway look.

"Did you both see it?"

Steve nodded. "Briefly. It all happened so fast. We'd found a clearing with a few interesting-looking holes. Mark and I were taking soil samples while Adriana was looking for more disturbances, and we heard her screaming. When we found her, some guy was on his hands and knees, biting her legs—"

"Adriana had fallen down and was fighting him off with a branch, but he was crazed. When the guy saw Steve and me running toward him, he ran off."

"Did you call Bevlov?" I asked.

The two men exchanged uneasy glances. Steve blinked behind his glasses.

"No. She'd have a fit if she found out we were up there. She doesn't know I've got other researchers helping me. In fact, I wasn't supposed to be in Chavez Ravine at all. I was supposed to be chasing some leads. Which I did already, and they went nowhere. The whole investigation is a big mess. My boss wants us looking for entities 2.0 while we have the chance, and Bevlov is fighting it—"

Mark interrupted again. "She thinks our whole department should be outsourced."

Of course she did. Bevlov was an old-school cop who thought crime was the city's number one problem. Public opinion polls had shown time and again that entities were at the top of that list, with potholes and traffic close behind.

I glanced at the double doors leading to the ER. "What did you tell the doctors?"

Mark grimaced. "Well, we kind of lied. We said she'd been attacked by an entity."

"Do you think it *was* an entity?" I asked, pacing in front of them.

"No," they said at the same time.

"I think you're right." I ran a hand through my hair. It was tangled and needed a wash.

Mark eyed me with open curiosity. "So, what do you think it was?"

"Something I need to deal with." I sighed, imagining the long night ahead of me. "I'd love to explain, but I better get going." I turned to Steve. "And I'm sorry. I'm sorry this happened, and I hope Adriana is going to be okay."

Steve frowned. "It's not your fault."

But it felt like it was.

Leo had fed the cat and spent quality time together snuggling on the couch. He had messaged me with photographic evidence of Sam's infidelity, which he knew made me jealous. Sam was never cozy with me like he was with Leo and Julia.

However, Sam was curious about the large plastic bin I had set on the coffee table. When I took the swords out and laid them down gently, Santa Muerte seemed to perk up too. I went into the sunroom and had a one-way chat with Little Lencha, updating her on El Cucuy and the swords.

After planting a kiss on top of her head, I went back into the living room, where Sam was sitting inside the crate, peering at me over the edge, his green eyes glinting.

I poured myself a glass of pinot grigio and flopped onto the couch, wondering how I was supposed to supercharge the swords. Perhaps I could whip up a chili dish using the magical habaneros growing in my backyard, but without Lencha's help, that wasn't likely to go anywhere.

No, I was on my own, stuck using whatever sporadic and mysterious magic I could muster.

Sam jumped out of the box and circled the coffee table, his tail high in the air.

"Hey, my mother says you're my familiar, so make yourself useful and tell me how we're supposed to turn those swords into Cucuy-killers."

Sam stopped abruptly. He swiveled his big head toward me. I sighed—I knew that look.

I fetched a bag of salmon nuggets and tossed one to the cat. Sam watched while it hit the floor right in front of him and skittered across the room. He turned to glare at me, sauntered over to the nugget, pushed it around with a paw, smelled it, then slowly put it in his mouth.

"I hope my offering was acceptable, Your Highness."

Sam licked his paws, jumped onto the end table, and pushed the box of Santa Muerte tarot cards over the edge. It landed on the floor with a dull thud and came open.

A card came shooting out of the box, face down.

I flipped it over. It was the Ace of Swords.

As much as it pained me to admit it, my mother might have been right about Sam.

"Good job." I tossed him a second nugget, then picked up the card and studied it.

A bony hand held a sword high in the air against a bright yellow sun, the wrist entangled with iridescent green vines.

I took a deep breath and focused on the card in my hands. My mother had said it symbolized the triumph of the intellect. I wanted to believe I was smarter than El Cucuy, but he had killed three people and had evaded me and Bevlov, so he was no dummy. And while he desperately wanted to be human, he was still more monster than man, with all the raw impulses and violence that entailed. I had human intelligence on my side, the ability to think logically, unencumbered by urges and distractions.

The card gave me strength. It felt like a powerful omen predicting my triumph over the being that had terrorized mankind for centuries.

I set the card aside and turned my attention back to Sam, who was eyeing me expectantly. "All right, buddy. Let's do this."

I propped the card against the figurine of Santa Muerte. Her eyes seemed to glitter. When I picked up the rapier Hernan had chosen for me, my hands felt hot and began to glow red just beneath the skin.

Sam's tail swished back and forth, and a surge of power electrified the air. The metal hummed under my touch. The table below Santa Muerte vibrated, and a faint yellow aura shimmered around her.

I set the sword down and picked up the next one. My hands grew hot and itchy, but I pushed aside the discomfort, concentrating on infusing the metal with magic, picturing a vortex of power enveloping the blade. The walls seemed to fall away. I was in a trance, not in control of my body, viewing the scene from above, picking up each sword one by one.

Words fell from my lips, asking Santa Muerte to give me the strength to rid Chavez Ravine of the evil presence waiting to strike again.

When I became aware of my surroundings, I was swaying back and forth. Sam's heavy body was stretched across my feet, as if anchoring me to the floor. The mystical energy was gone from my hands.

The swords were neatly laid out on the coffee table. Each seemed to have gone through a transformation: their edges were razor-sharp, their blades freshly polished.

The figurine of Santa Muerte was motionless. She didn't wink an eye or flicker with inner light, and yet I could sense her approval settling over me like a heavy, comforting blanket.

I was exhausted, desperately in need of a shower and some sleep.

But I was ready to face El Cucuy.

Chapter 36

The next morning, the hot sun decided to take a break. Dark clouds rolled in, and by the time I left the house, rain was coming down in sheets. It was a summer storm—a rarity in Los Angeles.

While I briefed my team in the command center, it became clear this was no squall, but a full-on storm, complete with wind, lightning, and the most intense downpour I could remember.

The dramatic weather made it hard for my team to focus on swordcraft, but I wasn't too worried. Bailey, Justin, and Liam seemed to have a natural talent for it, just as they had for the slingshots. Ron struggled a bit, partly because he kept acting out scenes from action films.

He frowned at his sword. "Are you sure this has magic? It doesn't *feel* like it."

Bailey rolled her eyes. "Dude, don't expect miracles. You actually need to know how to use it."

"Harsh," he muttered.

Bailey pointed the tip of her sword at Ron, who flinched. "Quit showing off and focus on what you're doing."

I stayed out of it. Sometimes, peer pressure was more effective than a scolding from the boss.

Liam stood in a corner away from the others. With a plate-sized hand holding the hilt, he practiced thrusting at an imaginary opponent. With his rugged looks and broad shoulders, it was easy to imagine him wearing a Viking helmet, vanquishing whoever got in his way.

"This rain isn't letting up," he said, glancing out the window. "Do you think we should wait? It's going to be a muddy mess out there."

I shook my head. "No. He may use the storm as cover for his next attack. We can't afford to wait."

"I agree," Bailey said.

"So do I," Justin added.

Ron nodded. "Anyone have any rain gear they can loan me? I don't have any."

Liam shook his head. "I used to have rain jackets and stuff back when I lived in Portland, but I tossed them when I realized it hardly ever rains here."

We couldn't very well set out for Phantom's Pass without proper gear. I thought for a moment. "Isn't there a military surplus store down the street from the Bishop gate?"

Ron grinned. "Yeah, there is. That's where Brandon and I buy all our camo. It's huge. They've got everything in there."

It would be a quick detour. After packing up the swords, we headed out, taking my Jeep and the security vehicle with all-wheel drive.

Ron hadn't exaggerated. The military surplus store was much larger than it had appeared from the outside. We scooped up rain jackets, pants, waterproof boots, and a rain cover for the swords, just in case. I paid for everything using my work-issued credit card, and then we were on our way to Phantom's Pass.

Our gear smelled of plastic, but the jackets had high collars and built-in brims on their hoods, helping to keep the rain out of our eyes.

The wind howled through Chavez Ravine, like the banshees that had invaded Laurel Canyon a few months before. We plodded up the path where Adriana from Occult Affairs had been attacked. Lightning split the sky. Bailey was just ahead of me, her head down, boots splashing through puddles as we trudged toward our destination.

The rain began to fall even harder, and the wind picked up, roaring through the trees. Everything was a blur of water and noise. At one point, Bailey slipped and fell in the mud, and then I did the same, but we managed to keep a steady pace, pushing forward against the chaos of the storm.

Despite the noise, we remained quiet, talking in whispers.

When we reached a fork in the trail, the group stopped.

"Which way, boss?" Ron asked.

Somehow, without the sun and birds, it looked different than it had with my mother.

I closed my eyes and tried to envision the path that would lead us to El Cucuy. A small light sparkled behind my left eye. Guidance from Santa Muerte? Or a migraine coming on?

"Left," I said, betting on the saint of death.

The rain was a constant drumbeat on my plastic hood. The backs of my heels hurt where they rubbed against the new, stiff boots. I would have a blister by the time I got home.

If I made it back.

We finally broke through a cluster of trees, and I held up my hand.

I wiped the drops from my eyes, scanning the rain-soaked clearing. Hairs lifted on the back of my neck. El Cucuy wasn't far. I could feel it. Was he watching us?

Liam opened the crate and handed me my sword. I was happy to have it in my hands again.

Ron stepped a few yards away from us, holding his weapon in front of him and peering around a large boulder.

I watched him, my heart hammering in my chest. "Get back here," I hissed.

A flash of lightning turned the world white, and in that fraction of a second, something moved in the corner of my vision.

Bailey, mouth slightly open, was looking at me while I stared at what was behind her.

"Move!" I screamed.

She whirled around, her sword raised.

El Cucuy had changed since the last time I had seen him. He was more human, bigger and taller, his pale face cross-hatched, as if it were made from bits of white cloth stitched together. A face in progress.

The others charged forward, slipping and sliding in the mud, and Bailey slashed at the Cucuy. The silver blade of her sword sliced through the air.

A boulder surrounded by pools of rainwater stood between me and the monster. Before I could make my way around it, El Cucuy had knocked the sword out of Bailey's hand. He lunged forward, grabbed her by the legs, and with lightning speed, dragged her away into the dense undergrowth.

Chapter 37

Justin, Liam, and Ron rushed past me and vanished into the brush. I followed, but my foot plunged into a muddy hole. Screaming in frustration, I yanked my foot free from the mud and stumbled forward, desperate to catch up with the others.

The mud in my boot squelched while I ran. The dense foliage seemed to close in, slowing my progress. The onslaught of rain made it impossible to see far ahead. I had no idea which direction my team had gone. Though I paused for a moment to listen for them, the roaring wind was the only sound in my ears.

A moment later, a break in the trees revealed a small clearing, where Justin, Liam, and Ron stood, their backs to me.

Somehow, everyone—including me—had managed to hold onto their swords. Justin held two: he must have picked up Bailey's.

I joined them, a ball of a panic in my throat making it hard to breathe.

El Cucuy had left a trail of footprints. Justin pointed at deep grooves in the mud next to them.

"Drag marks."

"Looks like she fought like hell," Liam said through gritted teeth.

"Shit, shit, shit." Ron groaned. "Now what are we going to do?"

We were standing before what appeared to be the entrance to a cave, one partially obscured by a tangle of tree branches.

Liam stepped forward and threw aside the largest limb. The rain continued to fall in a curtain around us. The faint, watery light was no match against the blackness within.

"Does anyone have a flashlight?" I asked, already knowing the answer.

No one even bothered to search their backpacks.

"I can run back and grab some from the cars," Ron offered.

I shook my head. "It'll take too long. We've got to go in now. Before he…" I couldn't even say the words.

The sword in my hand answered with a slight vibration.

"You guys stay here. I'm going in."

"That's a bad idea, boss," Ron said.

Justin touched my elbow. "For once, I agree with him." He took a few steps toward the mouth of the cave and peered inside. "It's pitch-black in there. You won't be able to see a thing. You can fall and break your neck."

"It could be a trap," Liam said. "That fucker could be waiting just inside, and you wouldn't know what hit you."

I sighed. Probably. But I couldn't just stand there and do nothing. Besides, I was the one with the magic. "I've got to try. You stay here. No use all of us getting ambushed, if that's what he has in mind."

I stepped toward the cave, but someone tugged the back of my jacket. When I turned, Liam was staring down at me, his heavy brow furrowed.

"I want to go too."

I pulled free and raised my sword. "I might have more luck if I'm alone. If I can focus."

"On magic?" Liam's scowl deepened.

"Something like that." I didn't know if I believed it myself or if it was just a convenient excuse to keep them safe. "Whatever you do, don't call after me. We don't want to let him know I'm coming."

Three heads nodded reluctantly.

I stepped across the threshold and into darkness. The noise of the storm followed me, but not for long. The sword thrummed in my hand. Despite the gloom, I could make out the path ahead. I glanced down at my sword. It was glowing.

The illumination was faint, but it was enough that I could see the ground directly ahead of me and, to my left, a rock wall. I took another few cautious steps, gripping the hilt of the sword with both hands. As I crept forward, the gleam from the silver blade increased.

By the time I reached a sharp turn, my sword was better than a lantern or flashlight. It lit up the entire cave so I could move quickly around several abrupt corners.

With the sound of the storm in the distance, it was easy to lose track of time and space. I couldn't have been inside more than a few minutes, but it felt like an hour had gone by, and I hoped whatever magic had lit up my sword wouldn't fail. My hands trembled at the mere thought.

A familiar smell—wet dog combined with rotting flesh—filled the air. Something crunched under my boot. It was a bone. A long one that had been badly gnawed by a set of nasty teeth. My stomach lurched. I held out my sword, revealing more bones littering the ground, which I picked my way around. My neck felt like it was made of metal rods.

I rounded another corner, entered a large chamber, and nearly screamed.

El Cucuy was pressed against the far wall. His pale face seemed to float, and for one horrible moment, I thought he was airborne. But it was just a trick of the light. I looked around for Bailey, and eventually, I found her, trussed up in some sort of cocoon made of filthy cloth suspended from the ceiling. She was moving.

"I'm here, Bailey," I said quietly.

Desperate wriggling from the cocoon.

El Cucuy regarded me silently. He was a terrifying sight. The stuff of childhood nightmares. His eyes were pools of darkness radiating menace and hunger.

The silence of the chamber was broken only by Bailey's muffled cries, which echoed off the walls.

I raised my sword. Its light cast strange shadows on the walls. El Cucuy stepped sideways and growled. His shape skewed and contorted, and a dark power emanated from him, which made my blood run cold.

If it hadn't been for Bailey, I might have turned around and run, but I couldn't back down. She was coming out with me, no matter what.

I thought of all the people who were counting on me to keep them safe and the three people he had killed. Thought of my team, including the three waiting at the mouth of the cave. Images of my friends, my cat, Stu, and Clare flashed before me. A rage boiled in my gut, rising through my chest, and with a hoarse battle cry, I charged ahead.

El Cucuy roared and lunged toward me, mouth open wide, clawed hands outstretched.

I dodged to the side just in time, feeling the rush of air when he hurtled past me and slammed into a wall.

With a surge of adrenaline, I swung my sword in a wide arc, aiming for the side of his neck. But instead of slicing through his flesh, the blade bounced off it. The Cucuy spun around, his pale face twisted with rage, and advanced toward me once more. I was vaguely aware of Bailey screaming.

Taking a step back, I raised my sword again, silently appealing to Santa Muerte for help against this horrible evil. The hilt of my rapier hummed in response, and my heart soared, but the next moment, the blade flickered and grew dim.

No. Please, no. Not now. Santa Muerte? Can you hear me?

The monster paused, his head cocked in interest. Was he some sort of mind reader?

I tried to force my thoughts to go blank. Instead, my consciousness refused to cooperate. It called out for Santa Muerte, to my great-aunt Lencha, to my grandmother Lily, to the spirits who might help me in my hour of need.

El Cucuy seemed frozen, mesmerized.

All the while, my sword continued to dim. In a matter of moments, I would be plunged into darkness. El Cucuy would have the advantage. He was a creature of the night, experienced at stealing children from their beds, and he would win.

I wanted to cry. To scream. My sword had failed me. It should have sliced off the monster's head. The weapon was made of the strongest Toledo Steel. Even on its own, it should have gone through its flesh like a knife through soft butter. With my magical boost, El Cucuy's ugly head should have been rolling around at my feet. Which meant he was far more powerful than I had thought.

How could I have allowed myself to get into this situation? My whole life, I had relied on one person—me—to solve my problems. But when it came to brujería, I had come to depend on others, to assume they would come to my assistance. Because I had not completely trusted my new skills.

In a flash even brighter than the lightning streaking the sky outside, I understood. My mother and even Hernan had tried to warn me, but I had not listened. The help I needed could have only come from within.

"Dammit," I screamed into the darkness. I was furious. With myself. With my stubbornness, and my fear. And I was going to die, unable to protect my team or my neighbors.

A molten anger filled my chest. It coursed down my arms and heated my hands. The blade gave one final flicker, and we were plunged into darkness. A moment later, the tip of my sword erupted in flames.

It was like holding a flamethrower.

El Cucuy shrunk back.

I waved my new weapon at him. He flattened himself against a wall, cowering before the fire.

My despair was gone.

Like a master of the elements, able to conjure fire and banish evil beasts, I lunged at El Cucuy. The flames coming from my sword stretched to meet him. He rolled against the wall, hands over his head, trying to get away, but I wasn't going to let that happen. I aimed the fire at one shoulder and then the other, and when he whirled around, hands batting at the air, I plunged the sword deep into his chest.

There was a sizzling sound and a horrible, acrid stench. El Cucuy let out a guttural roar while the flames engulfed him. The hilt grew so hot I released my sword and backed away, watching and waiting. In a matter of seconds, the bellowing had stopped, and the writhing figure became still. I held my breath until there was nothing left of the monster but a pile of ash.

When I was sure El Cucuy was no more, I picked up the sword from the gritty mound and wiped it against my pants. The flame was gone, but the glow had returned.

Above me, Bailey had somehow poked her head out of the cocoon. I held the sword up so I could see her face.

She managed a weak smile. "I wish I could have seen that."

I smiled back and took a good look at her. Her signature eye makeup had finally met its match. The glittery gray shadow ringing her eyes had smudged over her nose and cheeks. It made her look like a racoon about to hit a night club.

"Are you all right?"

Bailey grunted. "I'll be better when I'm out of this thing. It stinks."

I handed her my sword and watched while she cut herself free. She dropped to the floor and, Bailey being Bailey, landed on her feet. We stared at each other for a moment, then she threw her arms around me and squeezed. I hugged her, patted her on the back, and gave her a friendly push toward the exit.

While we made our way out to the stormy woods, I felt myself smiling.

Not bad for a basic bruja.

Chapter 38

Detective Leesa Bevlov was not going to like it. In fact, she would hate it. But after everything I had been through, I just didn't care. In the slightest.

My number one priority was the Chavez Ravine community, and they deserved to know that the killer who had terrorized our town was dead.

We couldn't very well say an ancient monster had resurfaced and I had taken him out with a magical sword, so we had to be a little creative in the way we worded the announcement.

In my office, with a spiced latte fueling my fingers, I typed out my carefully worded message.

Greetings Chavez Ravine HOA members:

Following an internal investigation, Chavez Ravine Security has determined a rogue entity was responsible for the tragic deaths of three members of our community. The one-of-a-kind entity was captured and neutralized. I want to assure everyone this creature no longer poses any danger to the community.

I'd like to thank the members of our security team, who worked tirelessly to ensure the safety and well-being of our neighbors in Chavez Ravine. We remain committed to maintaining a secure environment for all. As always, please report any suspicious activity to our security team, and together, we will work to prevent any future threats.

We are not at liberty to disclose more details about the entity, as the matter is being taken up by the research division of LAPD's Occult Affairs group. Thank you for your understanding.

That last bit was somewhere between a truth and a lie.

Thanks to Steve Zhao acting as intermediary, the head of entity research had agreed to go along with this bit of fiction in exchange for us allowing Steve and his associates to continue their investigations for a few more weeks.

After meeting Steve and hearing his earnest guarantee his three-person team would share their findings and not overstep, even Cora and Hernan had thought it was a good idea.

Charlie Perez, who had grown up with the legend of El Cucuy, had nonetheless been stunned to learn the monster was real. The two other board members, Eileen Simpson and Dan Berman, were told the "rogue entity" story.

Sometimes, the board operated as a whole. Occasionally, it split along cultural lines.

After the board approved the message in an emergency session, I asked Cora if she wanted to send it out herself.

"Oh my, no. It should come from you. You sent the alerts, even though you knew they wouldn't be popular with everyone, and now you should take the credit for solving the problem."

I went back to my office and hit send. A sense of relief washed over me. My office became bathed in a golden glow. The storm had passed, and the sun broke through the dark clouds, as if matching my mood. I opened the window and breathed in the fresh, clean air.

Closing my eyes for a moment, I basked in the warmth of the sun against my skin. My neck and shoulders had relaxed, but I still had plenty of things to do before my long day was done.

Ron, Bailey, Justin, and Liam had agreed to keep the story of El Cucuy to themselves. We didn't dare risk the truth getting out, knowing the panic it would cause among the Latino residents. If they realized El Cucuy had been real, what other childhood nightmares might show up in Chavez Ravine? La Llorona, the legendary weeping woman?

At home, I fed Sam and headed straight for a long, hot shower. My shower gel couldn't get rid of the clinging odor of El Cucuy, so I dragged an exfoliating glove slathered with vanilla-scented sugar scrub against my skin until it was bright pink. Then I washed my hair. Twice.

Sam joined me in the bathroom and made himself useful by swatting around a lipstick tube on the tile floor.

I dressed in shorts and a tank top, then tidied up the house. In the kitchen, I inventoried the cupboards and pantry, thinking of what I would prepare for Stu when he came home. He had agreed to be my plus-one at a little celebration Cora had arranged at Muertos Café for the next night, and I was counting on him staying over.

I had planned on a special, welcome-home breakfast. Machaca con huevos. As a meat lover, he would appreciate that.

After the storm, my garden needed tending. I went outside, pinched off some dead leaves from the potted plants, and swept the small patio. In the sunroom, I dusted the workbench while I filled Little Lencha in on what had happened with El Cucuy.

She had no reaction. Not even a flicker.

My throat suddenly went scratchy.

"I hope, wherever you are, you are at peace," I whispered. "And thank you for everything you've done for me."

The serious figure of Santa Muerte waited silently for me in the living room.

I pressed my hands together and gave a little bow. "Thank you for showing me the way."

Santa Muerte hadn't supercharged the Toledo Swords as I had hoped, but she had given me something far more important—the ability to take responsibility for my own magic. No more relying on outside sources. From now on, I would only rely on myself, as I always had before.

I stared at the sculpture. She was beautiful, regal, and imposing. The dark hollow orbits where eyes would have glimmered seemed to pierce through me.

As much as I appreciated all she had done for me, I couldn't imagine her staying in my home. I didn't think she would like sharing a humble wooden workbench with Little Lencha. Santa Muerte deserved an altar all her own, and that would raise lots of questions whenever someone visited.

Julia would love her, but that didn't seem right either.

Suddenly, I had it. I knew exactly who would appreciate her. Besides, I needed to return his precious Toledo Swords.

For once, Hernan greeted me at the door instead of Marta. He had given her a rare day off, he explained. Hernan was spiffed up, wearing dark blue linen trousers and a crisp white short-sleeved shirt. His black hair was combed back and appeared slightly wet, as if he had overdone the gel. He smelled good too. Like expensive aftershave.

I carried the plastic bin with two boxes balanced on top. After handing him the one containing the pan dulce I had picked up at Muertos Café, I followed him inside, carrying the bin and the other one.

"What a treat!" he said over his shoulder. He sounded pleased to see me.

In the living room, another surprise. The drapes were open, allowing the sunlight to pour in. The place was hardly recognizable. Even the dark furniture seemed happier. The wood gleamed with polish, and was that a new rug on the floor? It was patterned after a Mexican serape, done in brightly colored stripes. It reminded me of something Julia might have picked out.

There were other changes too: a gauzy white cotton throw draped across a couch, a pair of bejeweled gold sandals.

Alarm bells began to ring.

Someone was moving around in the kitchen. Then I caught Hernan watching me stare at the sandals.

"Um…"

That was as far as he got. The next moment, my mother appeared, holding two bottles of Mexican beer.

"Oh, mija, it's you! I was wondering who that was."

My lips opened and closed like a fish. When I found my voice, the words came out like I had a mouth full of marbles. "What are you doing here?"

My mother huffed. "Hernan invited me."

"I did." A flush crept up his neck. "I thought it would be nice to, you know, talk about our life experiences. We have so much in common."

Ah, the power of puppy love. Hernan had certainly changed his tune about my mother. In the blink of an eye, she had gone from mystical charlatan to charming lady friend. I just hoped that was all.

My mother's pedicured feet were bare under her long white caftan, gold braid trimming the deep V-neck showing off her tanned cleavage. Her hair was loose too. The alarm bells were clanging louder than ever.

I cleared my throat. "Aren't you worried my mother will attract entities?"

"Not at all," Hernan said breezily, then smiled. "I trust your spell will keep them away."

Spoken like a man who wanted to get inside my mother's caftan.

They were both adults. My mother hadn't had a relationship, as far as I knew, since she had dumped my father. And she could do worse than Hernan Frias. He seemed to have money enough, and he owned his home. Plus, he had a full head of hair.

My mother bustled into the kitchen and came back with another beer, which she set on the low coffee table.

I dropped into the closest easy chair and sipped my beer while the two settled onto the couch, their hips nearly touching. Placing the bottle on the floor next to my feet, I lifted the small box onto my lap, removed the lid, and pulled away the tissue paper.

"I'd like you to have this," I said to Hernan.

My mother scowled. "But it was a gift! To you."

"Yes, and I appreciated it, but I think she belongs here," I said firmly. I gently put her on the coffee table, facing Hernan.

He blinked and reached out a hand to touch her bony shoulder. His expression had become almost reverent. "If you're sure," he finally said, "I would be happy to welcome her into my home." He turned to my mother. "Where do you think we should put her?"

I nearly choked. "We?"

My mother glanced around the room, then pointed at a console table against the far wall. "She would look nice over there, don't you think? There's a place I know downtown where we can get some things to make her a proper altar."

Hernan nodded eagerly. "That would be wonderful. A gold cloth would be nice."

Good Lord. They had already reached the decorating together phase.

I reached down and tapped the top of the crate. "Thank you for loaning me the swords. I gave them a good cleaning." I paused. "Especially the one I used."

I hadn't mentioned the fire that had come out of the blade or how I had used it to incinerate El Cucuy. Hernan seemed satisfied knowing his Toledo blades had killed the monster stalking Chavez Ravine.

But I felt very tired. "Well, I better get going." I was sure that sounded awkward.

My mother stood up, her caftan billowing around her like a white, silky cloud. She clapped her hands together. "I think it's just amazing what you've accomplished." She gazed down at Hernan. "Isn't it amazing? That my daughter has vanquished El Cucuy, once and for all?"

Hernan frowned, then gave a little shrug.

We both stared at him. My mother pinched her lips. Hernan shifted on the couch like it was made of rocks.

"Hernan? That's amazing, right?" my mother said again.

He cleared his throat. "Well, yes, it's wonderful that Madeline killed El Cucuy. But he's not the only one."

My mother's eyes snapped wide. "What do you mean?" Her tone was sharp and demanding.

"I mean," Hernan began slowly, "there are others *like* him. It's something I found out while I was doing my research to help Madeline. El Cucuy is called into being by the parents who say his name to frighten their children. Some scholars believe, each time he is called, he is summoned anew. There's no telling how many Cucuys are out there."

My heart turned into a block of ice. The idea of countless Cucuys in the world sent chills down my spine.

My mother's face had paled. "That's impossible. It can't be true." Her voice was barely above a whisper.

Hernan reached up and took her hand. "I wish I could say otherwise, but that may be the truth."

The weight of Hernan's revelation followed me all the way home, where I discovered Julia waiting for me on the porch, sitting on an Adirondack chair and drinking a glass of wine. My neighbor Leo rested in the other. Both wore linen shorts. Julia had on a black tank top, but Leo hadn't bothered to change out of his blue Oxford shirt.

He held up a bottle of wine. "We couldn't wait, so we started early."

"We're here to celebrate you killing whatever it was you won't tell us about," Julia said.

"And we're here because you've been too busy and important to hang out with us," Leo added.

I took a deep breath and shook off all thoughts of El Cucuy. If there were others out there, I sincerely hoped there would be other Maddy Madrigals to take care of them.

I sank onto the top step and leaned against Julia's leg. She massaged my shoulders while Leo pushed a glass of wine into my hands. My gaze drifted to the townhouse across the street, where Naomi had died at the hands of El Cucuy.

I wished I had killed that sucker sooner, but I had done my best.

While I sat there with my friends, the stress of the previous weeks began to wane. No matter how many demons awaited in the shadows, I wasn't facing them alone anymore. I had friends, a boyfriend, a community, and a cat.

As if on cue, Sam's big head appeared through the open window, and he meowed loudly. I was late with his dinner.

Chapter 39

Muertos Café only opened for dinner once a week, so when it did, it was packed. At night, it became an entirely different place, with string lights stretched across the patio and candles flickering on the tables in the dining room. Small and cozy. Reservations required.

Cora had reserved the entire patio for my team. The *whole* team, not just those who had braved Phantom's Pass with me, because Cora genuinely enjoyed rewarding people for good performance. She didn't distinguish between greeting residents at the gates, patrolling the neighborhood, monitoring for entities in the command center, or marching into Phantom's Pass to slay El Cucuy.

When I arrived, everyone appeared to be several drinks in. People were talking loudly over the music and laughing.

Bailey and her boyfriend, Malik, huddled in a corner. Cora's husband busted out a bottle of mezcal, and servers brought trays of carne guisada and chicken ranchero nachos just in time to soak up all the booze.

I kept looking at the door, waiting for Stu to arrive. His plane had been delayed, but I hoped he would make it before dinner started.

Cora sauntered over and touched my elbow. "You look very nice. New dress?"

"Thank you. It is."

Cora was observant. It was made of breezy black cotton with an empire waist and white embroidered flowers along the neckline. Not too low for a work event. But I was only fashionable from the ankles up. Blisters had broken out on my heels after tromping around in Phantom's Pass, so sneakers covered my unsightly bandages.

Cora nodded at Justin, Liam, and Ron knocking back shots. "It's nice to see Ron doing so well. Thank you for mentoring him. His grandma and I are old friends, and she's always worried about him. He struggled in school and didn't seem to have much ambition. And then you arrived, and now look at him." She paused, lowering her voice. "You didn't give him that promotion because of me, did you?"

I shook my head. "Absolutely not. He deserved it. I would never give someone a job they couldn't handle. He's a fast learner. And if he ever takes a wrong step, he has those three to set him straight."

Cora chuckled. "Good. I'm glad to hear it." She glanced over her shoulder. "I'm off to the ladies while there's no line."

I had just accepted a glass of sparkling wine from a server when someone tapped my shoulder. It was Becca Tey, accompanied by Didi, her film editor friend. Becca wore a shimmery green maxi dress that reminded me of a mermaid, while Didi wore white jeans and a black *Phantom's Pass* crew T-shirt.

"We're about to have dinner inside and thought we'd come and say hello," Becca explained.

"Well, hello," I said. "It's great to see you both."

"Becca told me about the message you sent to your residents." Didi frowned. "So that thing we saw in the footage? You think *that* was the rogue entity?"

My face felt frozen. "Yep."

Didi grimaced. "Well, I'm glad you neutralized it, whatever that means. After all the buzz the movie has gotten, they're already talking about a sequel. I can't say I'm all that excited about it, after everything that's happened. It seems kind of ghoulish, you know?"

"Never turn down work." Becca waved a finger at Didi. "Especially not at our age, not in this damn business."

Didi sighed. "I wish I didn't love it as much as I do. My husband keeps telling me I should quit. We could sell up and move closer to his family in South Carolina—"

Becca interrupted. "And trade entities for hurricanes? No, thank you."

"Yeah, I'm not ready to do that," Didi continued. "I've still got a good five years before I'm ready to pack it in."

Becca poked Didi's arm. "Tell Maddy about what happened with that scene."

Didi leaned in, her eyes widening. "It was so weird. Yesterday, I was recutting the scene with that thing in the background. The director wanted me to blow it up so we could see it better. He was going to talk about it on the press tour. He'd already leaked it in some interviews, said viewers should expect something big. But when I started working on it, it was gone.

"At first, I thought maybe I was looking at the wrong take, but it was the right one. I even called in my assistant to check it out, hoping I'd made some kind of mistake. But no. She confirmed the figure had completely vanished."

I didn't know a thing about editing. "Could someone have deleted the figure somehow?"

Didi shook her head. "No. You can remove it with special effects, but not on the original footage I was working with. None of it makes sense."

It did to me. "What time did you notice he was gone?"

Didi's unplucked brow furrowed in thought. "I don't know. Four o'clock maybe? I'd just come back from the snack bar with a coffee."

I glanced around the bustling patio. The nachos were long gone. Through the plate glass, I watched Cora inside, talking with a group of people.

"Well," I began slowly, "that's about the time we took out our entity. Maybe there's some kind of connection." I figured I had better stop there or I'd find myself in a conversation I didn't want to have.

Becca and Didi exchanged a surprised glance. Didi spoke first, her voice hushed.

"Wow. That makes a strange kind of sense, actually."

"I need a drink." Becca pulled Didi toward the dining room. "Let's get together sometime soon, just the three of us," she said over her shoulder. "I'm buying."

After they left, I scrolled through my phone until I found what I was looking for. Sure enough, the image I had taken of the Cucuy in Didi's edit room was also gone.

Several servers came out, loaded down with trays of food.

Ron waved me over. "Boss, I saved you a seat."

"Suck up," Bailey said across the table.

I chuckled and headed in their direction. Just as I sat down, my phone chimed. It was Stu.

Almost there, babe.

Babe. That was nice.

I unfolded the red cloth napkin, placed it on the empty plate next to me to show the spot was taken, then turned to Malik.

"So, how are things back at the farm?"

Before he could answer, a figure in a garish jacket appeared behind him. It was Detective Leesa Bevlov, her lips pressed into a thin line.

I rose. "Detective, what a surprise." I tried to keep my tone light, but I was pretty sure I had failed.

Bevlov rolled her eyes. "Not as surprised as *I* was to hear your bullshit story about a rogue entity."

Everyone turned to stare. Bevlov's voice grew louder.

"I don't know what you think you're doing, but I'm in the middle of an investigation, and this case isn't solved until *I say* it's solved. If you want to feed your community a load of bullshit, that's up to you, but I'm just warning you…I'm about to issue a press release denouncing your claims as false."

My neck and face felt like they were on fire. I took a deep breath, trying to maintain my composure. "I understand your skepticism, but I assure you, it *was* a rogue entity."

"Damn straight!" Bailey said loudly.

Bevlov's gaze flickered to Bailey, sizing her up. "Save it. You worked for LAPD. You should know better. A human monster did this, not some freaky gnome. Entities aren't smart enough to stalk their victims or break into homes."

The chatter around us had died down to a hush. Bevlov's words echoed through the patio. My hands balled into fists, but I needed to let it go.

Bevlov had interrupted our dinner and said her piece. It was time for her to leave. Opening my mouth would have just prolonged the exchange, so I lifted my chin and said nothing.

Bevlov's nostrils flared, and she crossed her arms in front of her chest.

Not the stance of a woman about to leave.

"It's so typical of you to be sitting here, drinking and having a good time, instead of doing your job, protecting the community, while a cold-blooded killer is out there. It's a wonder you got the job at all, given your lackluster attitude and complete lack of credentials—"

"Leesa Bevlov, you should be ashamed of yourself!" Cora thundered behind her. "This behavior, this *atrocious*, disrespectful behavior, is the reason you did not get the security chief job. *Exactly this.* You do not possess one quarter of Madeline's skills. And you have none of her tact. Here in Chavez Ravine, we treat each other with respect. We resolve our differences like adults. And we don't tolerate insults and accusations from outsiders." Cora's dark eyes glittered with fury.

Bevlov paled and took a step back. Cora continued.

"You wouldn't have lasted two weeks in this job. I could see that a mile away."

I had never seen Cora so angry.

For once, Bevlov didn't have a snappy comeback. She seemed to crumple in on herself. I half expected her to drop to all fours and skitter away.

Cora pointed at the exit sign. "I believe your business here is done. Leave us to enjoy our meal celebrating the elimination of the murdering entity."

Bevlov's face flushed. With a curt nod to Cora and a sneer at me, she spun on her heel and marched out into the night.

Chapter 40

The tension that had gripped the patio released like air rushing out of a balloon. I hurried around the table and took Cora's warm hands in my own.

"Thank you for that."

Cora pulled me in for a hug. She smelled of jasmine and vanilla. "No need to thank me. No one messes with my team." She gave a little laugh when she released me. "And besides, I never could stand that woman."

That made two of us.

We dug into our dishes—carne asada and yucca fries with cilantro sauce. It took a while, but eventually, my muscles relaxed once again, and I sank back into my seat, feeling nothing but relief.

A second glass of sparkling wine helped too.

Stu made it just as dessert—chili-infused chocolate flourless cake—was being served. Cora asked a waiter to bring him a plate of food.

If I hadn't been surrounded by my co-workers, I would have jumped up and hugged him, but instead, I smiled and gave a little wave. He squeezed my shoulders before sitting down. The wine had gone to my head, and I wanted to pull him into a dark corner and do things to him, but instead, I grabbed his hand and kissed his knuckles. Across from us, Bailey smirked.

Once dessert was done, the waiters began clearing the tables. Cora said her goodbyes and paid the bill. Some of my team members talked about moving the party to Olga's Cantina, which stayed open until midnight.

"You're not coming?" Ron asked.

I sighed. "I don't bounce back like I used to, and I've got a full day tomorrow. But thanks. You kids go on ahead."

Ron scoffed. "Kids? You're not *that* much older." He looked Stu up and down, then raised his eyebrows. "Ah, okay. But if you change your mind, you know where to find us."

And then we were alone under the twinkling lights of the patio. The server came out with two glasses of Port.

"I saw your note about the rogue entity, but I heard Ron and Justin whispering about a cuckoo, or something. What's that about?"

I stared at Stu, wondering where to begin. There was so much I hadn't told him. About the supernatural history of Chavez Ravine. About my magical legacy. About what I had managed to achieve so far. If I were to start, I would be talking nonstop through the night, and I had other things on my mind. Like Stu's weirdly sexy wrists and the crinkles around his blue eyes.

I touched the side of his face. "How do you feel about walking home?" It was a beautiful, warm night, and it would give us a chance to talk.

"My place or yours?" He leaned in for a kiss, his lips warm on mine.

"Mine. It's closer."

Stu jumped up and pulled my chair away from the table, me along with it. "Wait, what kind of shoes are you wearing?"

How could I not love a man concerned about footwear? I held up a white sneaker. "They're cute but comfy."

Stu grabbed my hands and hauled me to my feet. "Let's go, then." Outside, he slung an arm around my shoulder. "God, I've

237

missed you. If I ever do a guys trip again, it will be a quick getaway weekend."

I leaned into Stu's side while we walked. "I missed you too."

He squeezed my shoulder. "A couple of days into the trip, I even started to miss being attacked by your cat. I thought, you know, I can't wait to get back and see Sam again. See which patch of skin he'll tear off next."

The night was quiet. The only sounds were our footsteps on the pavement and a few passing cars. We walked along the gravel path next to the gully.

"There are some things I need to tell you about," I finally said.

Stu stopped. "Oh? Did something happen while I was gone?" He seemed guarded.

"Lots happened, but all related to my job. And Chavez Ravine. And my family."

"Oh," Stu said again, relieved. "Well, I'm ready when you are."

I was ready. More than ready.

Fifteen minutes later, after Stu had said, "You're kidding," at least a dozen times, a strange noise in the distance reached my ears. It was a low, guttural rumble that seemed to vibrate through the very air around us.

I paused mid-step, my heart missing a beat. "Did you hear that?" I glanced around, trying to pinpoint the source of the sound.

"Yeah." Stu was looking around too.

The streetlamps in Chavez Ravine were tasteful but bright, and the moon was out, so we could see fairly well.

Something rose from the top of a nearby tree on a grassy hill. It was massive and dark, with wings that seemed to stretch out impossibly wide.

Stu stiffened. His hand gripped mine harder. "What the hell is that?"

"I don't know, but it doesn't belong here."

We watched the creature soar away into the distance, toward the hills of Elysian Park.

I called the command center. A new guard answered the phone.

"Command Center, this is Rafi."

"Rafi, I just saw something, but I'm not sure what. Are you seeing any signs of an entity in La Loma?" I asked, breathless.

"No, ma'am," Rafi said. "Let me refresh. One moment." A pause, then, "Still nothing, ma'am. If you can please send your coordinates, I will monitor the area and let you know if anything shows up. I'll check the feeds too."

Obviously, Rafi was on top of things, but I was still unsettled by what we had just seen.

Beside me, Stu sighed. "You can't seem to catch a break."

I felt that way too. My hands seemed to sense something was afoot in Chavez Ravine. They began to glow red.

Stu let go and gasped. "Is that...normal?"

"For me," I assured him.

I could see his face clearly in the moonlight. He nodded, and a smile lifted the corners of his mouth. "All right, then. I'm ready for a new normal, if you are."

To my surprise, I was.

We walked together, hand in hand, searching the sky for shadows but finding only the moon and stars. As we wound our way through the quiet streets of La Loma, the lingering presence of my ancestors followed us home.

Debra Castaneda

Author's Note

Thank you so much for reading *Desperate Magic!* The fourth book in the *Maddy Madrigal Mysteries* series, *Mortal Magic*, publishes this summer. I've planned for six books in the series, but there may be more. If you would like to receive updates, please join my newsletter and visit my website, DebraCastaneda.com, where I share the family recipes described in the novels and other fun stuff, too.

Now onto El Cucuy. He played a starring role in the nightmares of my childhood. While some kids today may fear movie monsters, like Pennywise, or the internet creepypasta sensation Slender Man, my East Los Angeles grandmother kept me in line with stories about the boogeyman of Latin American folklore.

The cucuy that eats children. Specifically, naughty children.

If he wasn't lurking nearby, there was La Llorona, the spectral ghost who wails for her dead children. In my grandmother's version, she was a wronged woman who drowned her kids, and she would get me, too, if I got too close. La Llorona worried me less because my grandmother didn't live near the water. But El Cucuy? He could be anywhere.

El Cucuy was a convenient way to scare kids into behaving, but he wouldn't work so well today. First off, terrifying children is a modern parenting no-no. Second, the kid would probably search for him online and quickly learn he's a myth.

But to me, El Cucuy is still scary, and I wrote about him as if he were real, though this time, he's hungry for adults. Of all the creatures that have appeared in the Maddy Madrigal series so far, El Cucuy is by far the most frightening predator.

Well, until book four. I think the creatures in *Mortal Magic* are deliciously creepy. But you'll have to be the judge.

More Books by Debra Castaneda

Maddy Madrigal Mysteries
Monsters, mayhem, and Mexican food

Barely Magic
Maddy lands a cushy security job in a gated community but must confront a supernatural threat and come to terms with her magical heritage.

Somewhat Magic
In the heart of Los Angeles, Maddy Madrigal battles legendary creatures and unscrupulous developers as an old protective spell begins to fail.

Desperate Magic
Maddy Madrigal must unravel a web of supernatural clues and confront ancient predators to stop a string of brutal murders.

Mortal Magic
Coming summer of 2025

Dark Earth Rising
Themed novels that can be read in any order

A Dark and Rising Tide
When a massive storm surge hits the central coast of California, the ferocious surf destroys buildings, floods streets, and washes up something sinister from the depths of the Monterey Bay.

The Devil's Shallows
Eight miles of mystery. One night of terror. Residents trapped in a remote neighborhood confront the unimaginable.

The Copper Man
Haunted tunnels. Unexplained deaths. Eerie sightings. Decades after The Copper Man killed her brother, Leah Shaw returns to the remote mining town of Tribulation Gulch where a lethal mystery awaits.

The Root Witch
A beautiful forest. A terrifying legend. It's 1986. Two strangers, hundreds of miles apart, grapple with disturbing incidents in a one-of-a-kind quaking aspen forest.

Circus at Devil's Landing
Creatures that howl in the night, a mysterious circus, and a clash between a ringmaster and a woman determined to rescue her captured lover.

Chavez Ravine Novels

Stand-alone novels set in Chavez Ravine, Los Angeles during turbulent times

The Monsters of Chavez Ravine

A 2021 International Latino Book Awards Gold Medal Winner! Before Dodger Stadium, dark forces terrorized Chavez Ravine.

The Night Lady

A rebel curandera, a plucky seamstress, and a young reporter are pulled into the investigation of a killer terrorizing Chavez Ravine.

The Haunting of Chavez Ravine

La Llorona is terrorizing people in the hills of Chavez Ravine, and a sassy curandera and her clever young niece must stop her.

The Christmas Cucuy

It's Christmas Eve, 1949, and Kiki's dreams are about to come true: she'll be singing at Palladium with her old bandmates. But when she threatens her rambunctious son with El Cucuy, her plans change.